A THING™ CALLED TRUTH

A THING CALLED TRUTH First Printing: April 2022 ISBN: 978-1-5343-2210-3

Published by Image Comics, Inc. Office of publication: P.O. Box 14457 Portland, OR 97293
International Rights/Foreign Licensing – Christine Meyer Christine @gfloydstudio.com

image® COMICS PRESENTS

A Shadowline® PRODUCTION

Co-Creators

Iolanda Zanfardino
Writer, Letterer, Covers

Elisa Romboli
Artist, Covers

Mirka Andolfo
Ivan Tao
Additional Covers

Melanie Hackett
Editor

Marc Lombardi
Communications

Jim Valentino
Publisher

Brett Evans
Production

Issue #4 Cover C by ELISA and IOLANDA
ROME
PARIS
LONDON

Issue #1 Cover A art by ELISA ROMBOLI

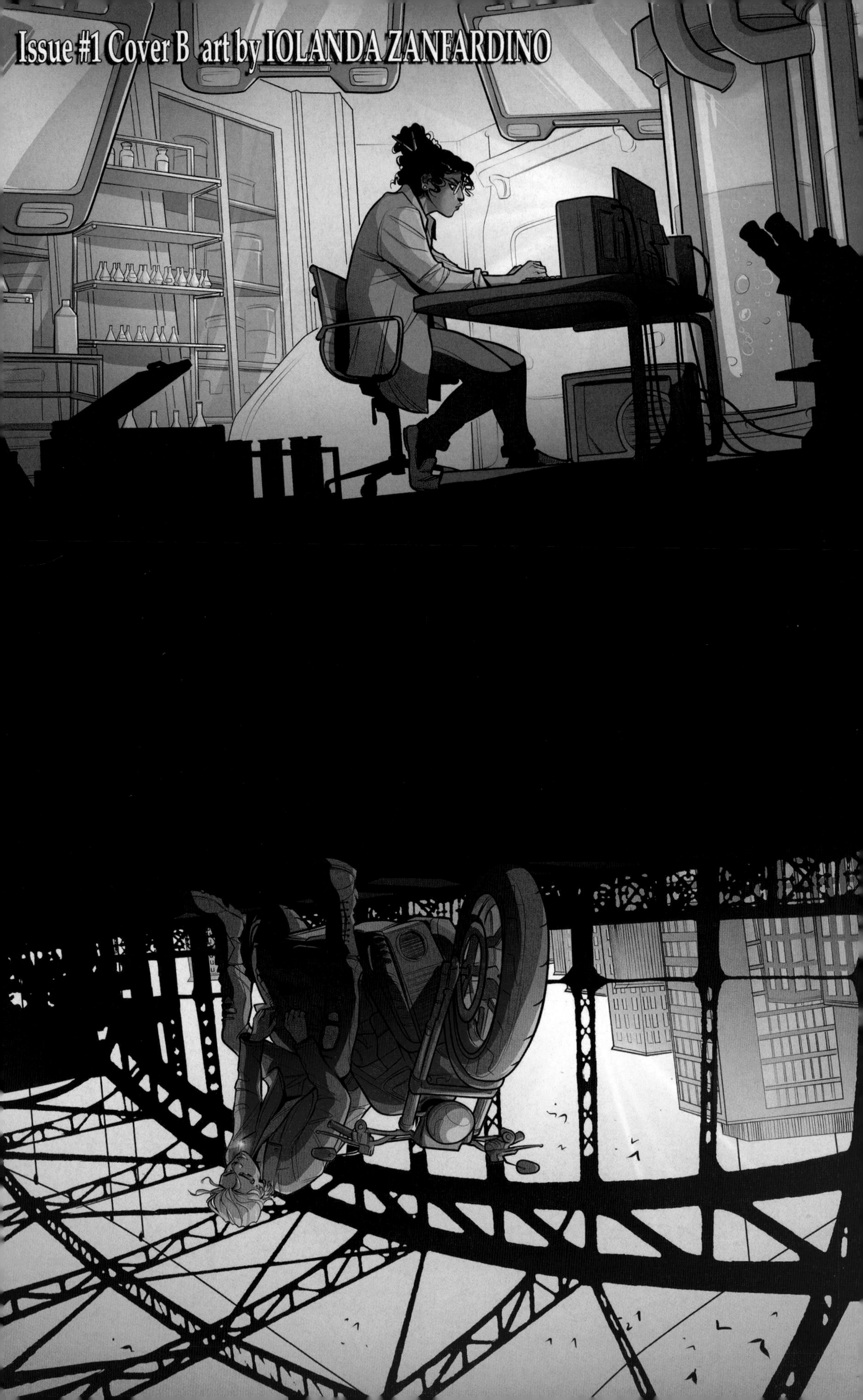
Issue #1 Cover B art by IOLANDA ZANFARDINO

VRROOOM
DOPPEL KREUZ PHARMA
FASTER! C'MON!!
SHIT! SHIT! SHIT!

WE'RE **NEVER** GONNA MAKE IT!
I'M NOT GOING BACK **NOW**!
HEART ATTACK. FROM WORK-RELATED STRESS.
TRIPPING AND FALLING DOWN FACE-FIRST IN THE LAB, LAUGHED AT ON SOCIAL MEDIAS.
OF OLD AGE. ALONE. FULL OF BITTERNESS. AND CATS.

CRACK
I THOUGHT I WAS GOING TO DIE EITHER ONE OF THESE WAYS.
INSTEAD--
HOW THE FUCK DID I GET INTO THIS MESS?

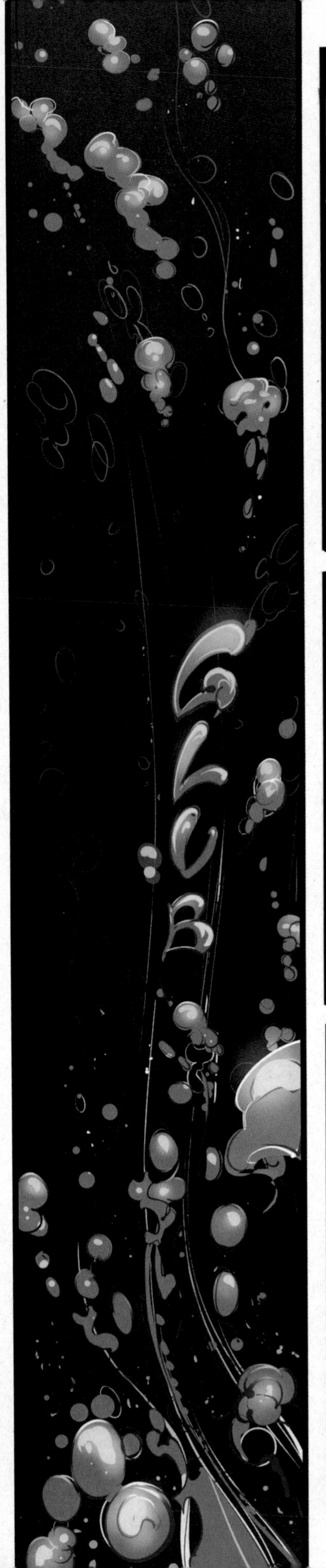

50
40

DAY 2136.

I'M DOCTOR MAGDALENE TRÄUMER. NEW DEVICES FOR SPECIALIZED MEDICINE RESEARCH AND DEVELOPMENT.

REC
THE LAST TESTS I'VE RUN HAVE BEEN **SUCCESSFUL**. THE DEVICES HAVE PROVEN TO BE EFFICIENT AND RESISTANT, EVEN THROUGHOUT CRUSH TESTS AND HIGH TEMPERATURE SIMULATIONS.

REC
THEY HAVE PROVEN SUITABLE TO MEET THE SPECIAL NEEDS OF HOSPITALS IN THE SOUTH OF THE WORLD. THEY ARE **FASTER AND MORE RELIABLE** THAN THE COMPETITOR'S.
AND THANKS TO THE NEW COMPONENT MATERIALS I TESTED, IT WILL BE POSSIBLE TO SELL THEM **FOR A TENTH** OF THE COMPETITOR'S PRICE.

WE WILL JUST NEED A FEW FINAL ADJUSTMENTS... TO FILE THE PATENT, AND WE WILL BE READY TO PUT THEM UP FOR SALE VERY SOON. THESE DEVICES WILL BE DEPENDABLE AND SO INEXPENSIVE **EVERY HOSPITAL** WILL BE ABLE TO AFFORD THEM.
WE CAN SAY THAT, IF PRODUCTION WILL MEET THE DEMAND, THEY COULD **SAVE THE WORLD**.

REC
THIS IS ALL FOR TODAY. IF I MAY BE OPTIMISTIC, THIS WILL BE ONE OF THE LAST RECORDINGS. **END OF THE VIDEO-DIARY**.

PHEW
THERE'S NEVER BEEN ANOTHER REASON TO BE ALIVE, FOR ME...
MAKE SOMETHING GOOD, LEAVE A SIGN.
I CAN DO IT. I CAN SAVE THE WORLD.
EVERY SACRIFICE I EVER MADE IS NOTHING COMPARED TO THE SENSATION OF BEING SO CLOSE...

AND FOR ONCE I CAN ALLOW MYSELF TO SLEEP AT HOME. BUT I CAN'T WAIT TO BE BACK HERE TOMORROW.
CLICK!

ALSO BECAUSE YOU KNOW... IT'S NOT LIKE IT'S SO THRILLING OUT THERE.
CLICK!
GHHH--
SHHWAFF
PAPERS TO SIGN
VERY URGENT
VERY URGENT
SIGN
PAPERS TO SIGN
VERY URGENT

WELL... UHMM.

OH...YEAH. I THINK IT IS FRIDAY NIGHT...?

DRIIIN DRIIIN
EX(ASPE-RATING) HUSBAND

UHM... YES, HELLO? DOCTOR TRÄUMER.
MAG. YOU KNOW **VERY WELL** WHO'S SPEAKING.
HEEEY. HI, NEVAL! HOW ARE YOU?
HOW'S THE EXPECTANT LADY?
MAG. THE **DIVORCE PAPERS**. DID YOU SIGN THEM? **FINALLY**?

SURE... EHM. I WILL, AS SOON AS POSSIBLE. I'M SO BUSY RIGHT NOW...
YES, AS YOU **ALWAYS** ARE. I SEE YOU AT THE COMPANY... ALWAYS BURIED IN THAT FUCKING BUNKER YOU CALL A PRIVATE LAB!
BUT I REALLY DON'T BELIEVE **ONE SIGNATURE** IS GONNA TAKE AWAY MORE THAN TWO MINUTES FROM YOUR NOBLE MISSION.
YEAH, I KNOW, I WAS ABOUT TO DO IT...
YOU'VE BEEN SAYING THAT **FOR MONTHS**!
DAMN, MAG, YOU HAVE TO-- **WE HAVE TO** LEAVE THIS WHOLE STORY BEHIND US.

IT'S JUST THAT I'M SO BUSY WITH MY NEW DEVICES, NEVAL! I'M **ALMOST** THERE, THIS TIME--
NO, **NO**! I DON"T WANNA HEAR IT! I WON'T HEAR ONE MORE WORD ABOUT THOSE FUCKING MACHINERIES THAT **RUINED OUR MARRIAGE**!

WAS IT **REALLY** ABOUT THAT? OR WAS IT ABOUT ME **NOT WANTING TO HAVE CHILDREN** WITH YOU, NEVAL?

WHY DO YOU HAVE TO BE LIKE THIS, MAG? YOU WERE NEVER WITH ME, YOU KNOW THAT.
YOU'RE A FUCKING GENIUS, YOU'RE THE BEST. BUT IT REALLY SEEMS LIKE YOU DON'T CARE AT ALL ABOUT... **LIFE**. THE LAST TIME I SAW YOU GO OUT TO GRAB A BEER, YOU WERE STILL IN YOUR PHD.
I-I...

ANYWAY. SEND ME THOSE PAPERS. OR LEAVE THEM ON MY DESK AT THE COMPANY. OR ASK THE **FUCKING CYBORG** YOU MUST HAVE HAD THE TIME TO BUILD IN YOUR LAB TO BRING THEM TO ME. BYE-
TOOT TOOT
TOOT - TOOT - TOOT
SIGH
GRAB A BEER... YEAH. LIKE THAT'S IMPORTANT...

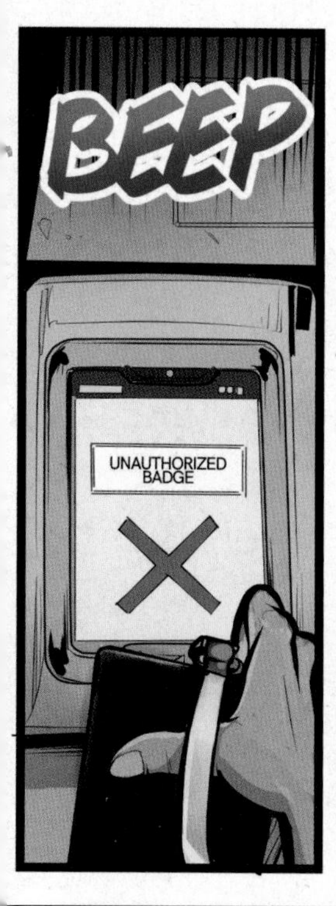
BEEP
UNAUTHORIZED BADGE

DOPPEL KREUZ PHARMA
MMMH... IT MUST BE BROKEN.
I'LL JUST LEAVE IT PARKED OUT HERE...

WUMPTH!

DOPPEL KREUZ PHARMA

ACCESS DENIED
WHAT--

BZZZ
TECHNICAL SUPPORT!
HELLO! UHM... THE BADGE READER NEEDS TO BE FIXED. IT DENIES ME ACCESS!
MH, MH. AND WHO ARE YOU?
WHAT-- WHO AM I?? I'M DOCTOR MAGDALENE TRÄUMER!
IF THIS IS A JOKE, YOU SHOULD KNOW I STRUGGLE WITH THIS KIND OF HUMAN INTERACTION...
MH, YEAH. IT IS PRETTY SIMPLE, DOCTOR. SINCE YOU RESIGNED YESTERDAY, YOU HAVE NO RIGHT TO ACCESS THE COMPANY BUILDING ANYMORE.
RESIGNED? WHAT??
I WOULD NEVER DO THAT! NOT NOW! THERE MUST BE A MISTAKE!
NO MISTAKE, MAGDALENE. YOU KNOW VERY WELL THAT VISITORS ARE NOT ALLOWED INSIDE ANY WORKING AREA AT THE COMPANY...
BOSS! CAN YOU TELL ME WHAT'S HAPPENING HERE??
I, MYSELF, ACCEPTED YOUR RESIGNATION YESTERDAY WHEN YOU CAME TO ME WITH YOUR PAPERS SIGNED, BEGGING ME TO DO SO!
WELL, EVERYONE COULD SEE YOU WERE A LITTLE... "UNBALANCED" LATELY. YOU DESERVE TO REST, MY DEAR.
DISMISSAL

W-WHAT... I DON'T...
IT'S M-- IT'S MY RESEARCH...
MY RESEARCH!! SEVEN YEARS I'VE BEEN WORKING ON IT!!
AND IT IS BY VIRTUE OF ALL THOSE EARS OF PEACEFUL COLLABORATION T WE WON'T INVESTIGATE WHERE AND W ALL THE FUNDS WE GRANTED YOU HAVE BEEN SPENT...
THOUGH, AS YOU POINTED OUT IN THESE PAPERS, YOUR RESEARCH CAME TO NO RESULTS.
BAM BAM
LET ME IN!! NOW! YOU CAN'T DO THIS!
YOU... ASSHOLES!! BASTARDS!!
AAAH, MAGDALENE. SO FRAGILE AND UNSTABLE, POOR DEAR. SECURITY WILL ACCOMPANY YOU TO THE MAIN ENTRANCE. YOU'RE IN SUCH A STATE YOU COULD EVEN GET LOST ON YOUR WAY OUT!
BEST WISHES FOR YOUR PERIOD OF REST, DOCTOR!
LET ME GO!!
THAT RESEARCH! COUNTLESS HUMAN LIVES ARE AT STAKE... LET ME GO!
YOU DON'T UNDERSTAND!!

DOPPEL KREUZ PHARM
EVERYTHING AS PLANNED, SIR.
SEE? I SAID SHE WOULDN'T BE MUCH OF A THREAT...
A TENTH OF THE COMPETITOR'S PRICE?
THAT'S AN IMPRESSIVE RESULT...
FILE NAME: Dr. Träumer (2011-2018)
ABSOLUTELY. PUTTING THOSE NEW DEVICES ON THE MARKET FOR A PRICE THAT'S ONLY SLIGHTLY LOWER THEN THEIRS WILL MAKE US THE RICHEST PHARMACEUTICAL COMPANY IN THE WORLD!
SIR, LET ME JUST SEND THE BOYS TO THAT FILTHY LAB TO DESTROY EVERY PROOF OF DOCTOR TRÄUMER'S INTELLECTUAL PROPERTY!
NOT THAT I BELIEVE ANY COURT OF JUSTICE WOULD GIVE HER CREDIT...

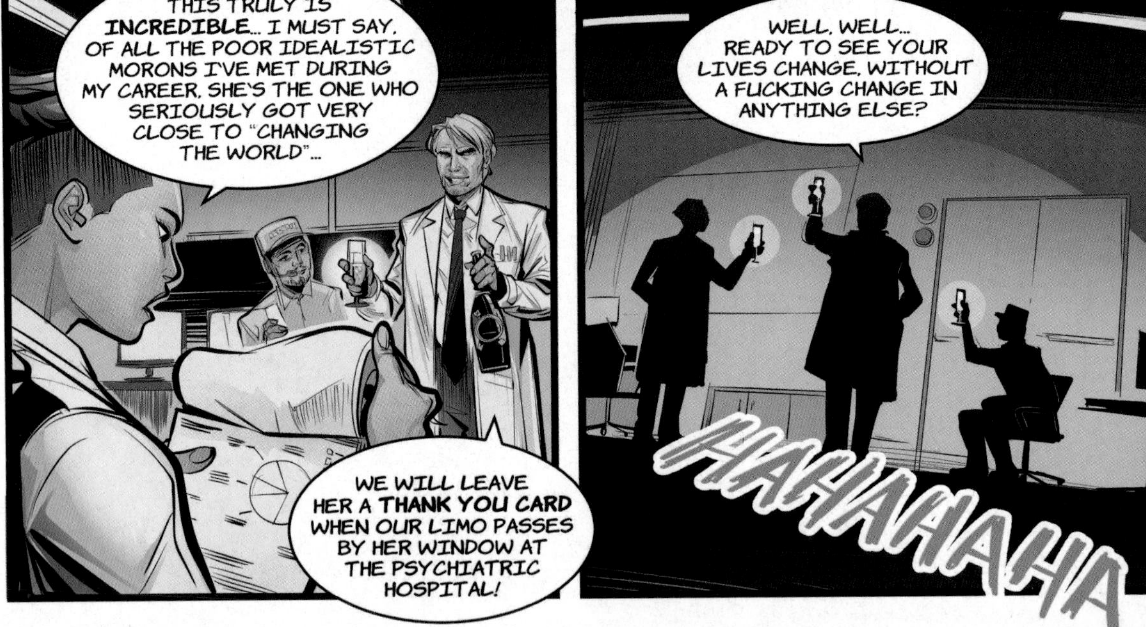
THIS TRULY IS INCREDIBLE... I MUST SAY, OF ALL THE POOR IDEALISTIC MORONS I'VE MET DURING MY CAREER, SHE'S THE ONE WHO SERIOUSLY GOT VERY CLOSE TO "CHANGING THE WORLD"...
WE WILL LEAVE HER A THANK YOU CARD WHEN OUR LIMO PASSES BY HER WINDOW AT THE PSYCHIATRIC HOSPITAL!
WELL, WELL... READY TO SEE YOUR LIVES CHANGE, WITHOUT A FUCKING CHANGE IN ANYTHING ELSE?
HAHAHAHAHA

WAITER!
I'M SORRY. COULD WE MOVE TO A TABLE FARTHER AWAY FROM THE BAR? REALLY TOO MUCH RACKET HERE!
O-OF COURSE! SO SORRY...
THEY LIE! THEY WANT TO MAKE ME LOOK LIKE I'M CRAZY!!
I'M NOT CRAZY, OK? I KNOW!!
WORD, SISTER!! I'M PERFECTLY SANE, TOO. I AM!
IT'S TRUE, THEY LIE!!
I KNOW, TOO! I KNOW!!
AND I WENT BACK THERE A THOUSAND TIMES, MY FRIENDS! THEY KICKED ME OUT AGAIN. A FUCKING PINBALL BALL!
POP!
A WHOLE LIFE SPENT IN THERE. I WAS SURE IT WAS WORTH IT!
YOU KNOW HOW LONG IT'S BEEN SINCE I GOT ME A NICE BEER?
ANOTHER BEER!!
BEEEEER!

BARMAN! ANOTHER ROUND. IT'S ON ME!
SLOW DOWN, DOCTOR. YOU DON'T LOOK LIKE YOU COULD STAND ANOTHER GLASS.
KIND MISTER BARMAN! I REMIND YOU I AM A GENIUS! I KNOW ALL THE EFFECTS OF ALCOHOL ON THE HUMAN BODY. AND MY PRESCRIPTION IS ANOOOOTHER GLASS!
SHE'S A GENIUS!
AN-O-THER-BEER! AN-O-THER-BEER!
SHE COULD HAVE SAVED THE WORLD!
TELL US AGAIN, DOCTOR!!
THIS IS THE LAST ONE, OK?
AND THIS IS THE LAST SATURDAY NIGHT SHIFT I AGREE TO DO. I SWEAR.
THE WORLD IS FULL OF CRUELTY, MY FRIENDS!
FULL OF MONSTROUS, SELFISH CREATURES!
AMEN, DOCTOR!
BUT WHAT DO YOU DO IF YOU STILL WANT TO SAVE IT?
MH??
DRIIN
EXASPERATING HUSBAND
FUCK OFF.

OOOHH
FRIENDS!
HEY! HEY! CALM DOWN NOW!
OOOOOHH
THIS MAN WHO WAS CALLING ON THE PHONE JUST NOW. THIS MAN ACCUSED ME OF BEING UNABLE TO ENJOY LIFE!
WELL, I'LL SHOW HIM! FROM NOW ON I WILL CONSTANTLY ENJOY LIFE!
MAGDALENE IS FREE! SHE CAN DO WHATEVER SHE WANTS!
YEEAH! LET'S SAVE THE WORLD TOPLESS!
WE LOVE YOU, DOCTOR!
WOOHOOO!
OK. ENOUGH NOW.

I TOLD YOU TO **CALM DOWN**, DOCTOR!
GO CATCH A BREATH OF FRESH AIR, AND NEVER SHOW YOUR FACE AGAIN AROUND HERE!

HEY!! SHOULDN'T YOUR JOB BE TO HELP AN **ESTEEMED PROFESSIONAL** IN HER MOMENT OF NEED?

AND ANOTHER THING...

I TOOK THIS! I **STOLE THIS**, Y'KNOW??
'CAUSE **I DRINK NOW**! THAT'S WHAT I DO! I'LL DRINK ALL NIGHT!
BRAUEREI
BRAUEREI

YECH.

UGH...
I DON'T THINK
I CAN DRIVE...

GOD...
COME ON,
MAG.

YOU'LL WAKE UP
AND FIND OUT THAT
THIS HORRIBLE DAY WAS
JUST A NIGHTMARE...

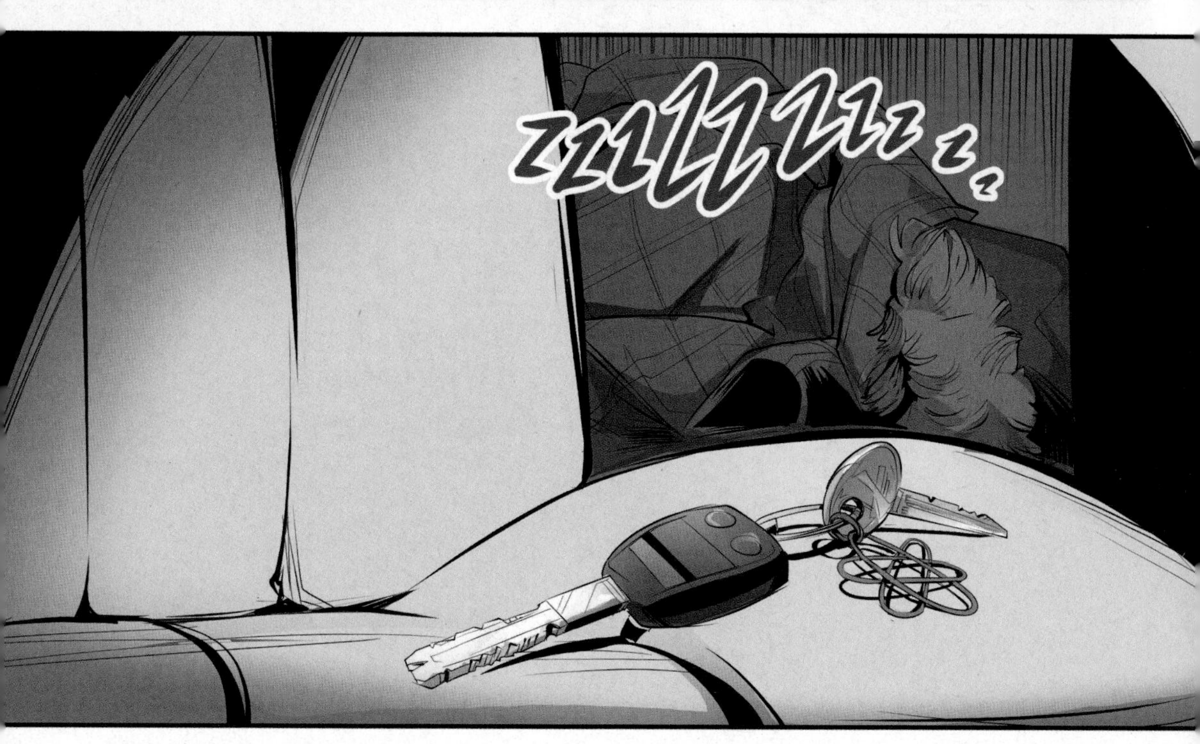
ZZZZZZZZZZ Z Z

MMHH...

MH??

WHA--

WHO THE FUCK ARE YOU??
AND WHAT THE FUCK ARE YOU DOING IN MY CAR??

OH, WOW, THERE WAS SOMEONE INSIDE THAT COCOON AFTER ALL.
ARE YOU A DOCTOR? WILL YOU PRESCRIBE YOURSELF SOMETHING FOR THAT HANGOVER?

DO YOU HAVE A TWENTY FOR GAS? WE'RE ALMOST OUT.

I'M CALLING THE POLICE!
TAKE ME BACK TO THE PUB AND GO AWAY, YOU-- YOU PSYCHO!
THAT WOULD TAKE QUITE A LOT OF TIME, DOC.
WE JUST ARRIVED IN ITALY.
... I-IN ITALY?-
WHAAAT?
W-WHAT KIND OF HALLUCINOGEN WAS IN THOSE BEERS??
THIS--... THIS CAN'T BE HAPPENING. YOU CAN'T BE REAL!

HAHAHA
I'M VERY REAL, DOC!
C'MON, COME SIT BY MY SIDE! WE STILL HAVE A LONG TRIP AHEAD OF US!
I'M NOT A DOCTOR, BUT IF YOU NEED SOMETHING FOR THE HEADACHE FEEL FREE TO RUMMAGE IN MY BAG!
A... TRIP?
D-DON'T LAUGH SO LOUD, PLEASE...
MY BRAIN IS EXPLODING...
AND WHERE THE FUCK IS MY PHONE??
GERMANY
IT WAS... THE STRANGEST THING TO WAKE UP TO. NOT EXACTLY WHAT YOU'D EXPECT WHEN YOU DECIDE TO EXIT YOUR COMFORT ZONE JUST FOR ONE NIGHT.
...AND IT WAS JUST THE BEGINNING.
AUSTRIA
ITALY
KINOKARTE

Issue #2 Cover A by IOLANDA ZANFARDINO

Issue #2 Cover B by ELISA ROMBOLI

HELLO. I'M DORIAN WILDFANG! I'M HERE FOR THE INTERVIEW.
OF COURSE I HAVE WORKING EXPERIENCE. I HAVE EXPERIENCE IN PRACTICALLY **EVERY FIELD**!
I CAN **DEFINITELY** WORK THE WEEKENDS!
CONSIDER US AVAILABLE FOR ANY PAID OVERTIME WHENEVER YOU NEED!
ABSOLUTELY! MY BROTHER AND I DO NEED THIS JOB!

GOOD EVENING!
HEY... IT'S "GOOD NIGHT" AT THIS POINT! WELCOME BACK.

HEY... HOW WAS MUM TONIGHT?
A BIT BETTER, I THINK...
SO, WHAT'S THAT FACE FOR?
NOTHING. NEVER MIND. HOW WAS WORK?

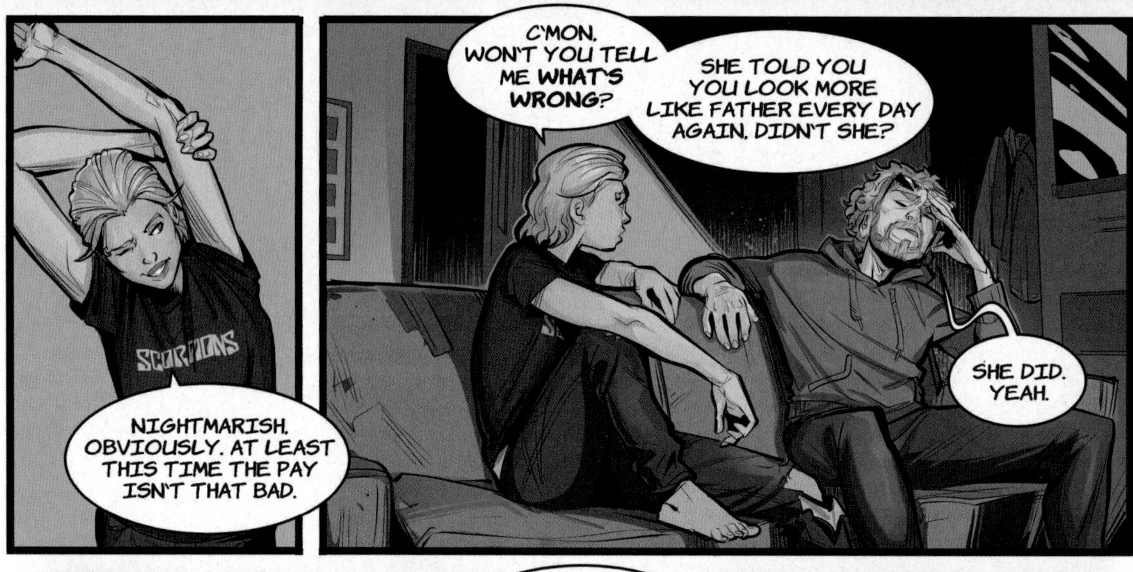
SCORPIONS
NIGHTMARISH, OBVIOUSLY. AT LEAST THIS TIME THE PAY ISN'T THAT BAD.
C'MON, WON'T YOU TELL ME WHAT'S WRONG?
SHE TOLD YOU YOU LOOK MORE LIKE FATHER EVERY DAY AGAIN, DIDN'T SHE?
SHE DID. YEAH.

IT'S JUST STUPID GENETICS, FAUST. IT'S JUST YOUR LOOKS. YOU WILL NEVER BE A PIECE OF SHIT LIKE HIM.
I KNOW, DORIAN.
THANKS.

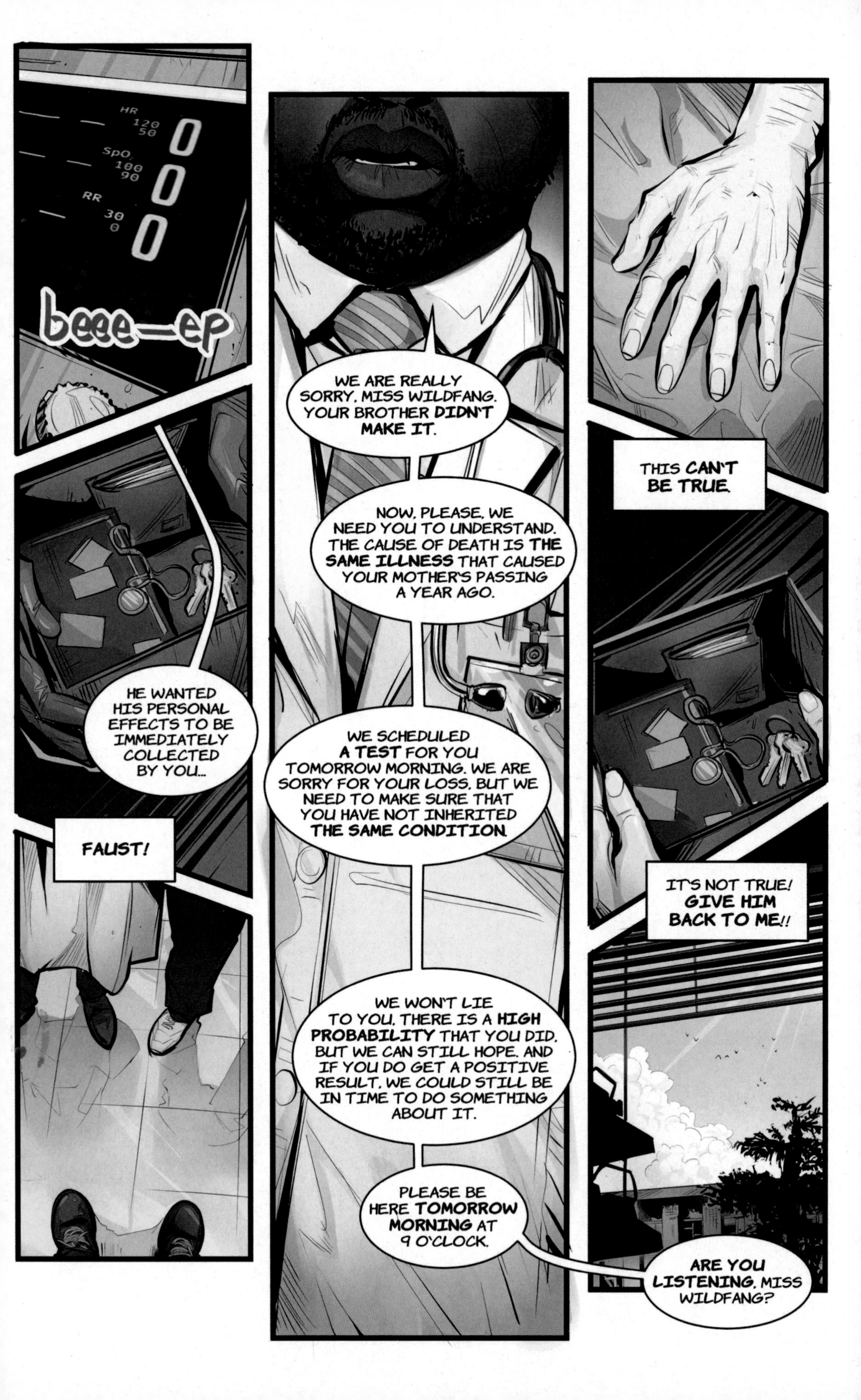
HR
120
50
0
SpO2
100
90
0
RR
30
0
0
beee—ep
HE WANTED HIS PERSONAL EFFECTS TO BE IMMEDIATELY COLLECTED BY YOU...
FAUST!
WE ARE REALLY SORRY, MISS WILDFANG. YOUR BROTHER DIDN'T MAKE IT.
NOW, PLEASE, WE NEED YOU TO UNDERSTAND. THE CAUSE OF DEATH IS THE SAME ILLNESS THAT CAUSED YOUR MOTHER'S PASSING A YEAR AGO.
WE SCHEDULED A TEST FOR YOU TOMORROW MORNING. WE ARE SORRY FOR YOUR LOSS, BUT WE NEED TO MAKE SURE THAT YOU HAVE NOT INHERITED THE SAME CONDITION.
WE WON'T LIE TO YOU, THERE IS A HIGH PROBABILITY THAT YOU DID, BUT WE CAN STILL HOPE. AND IF YOU DO GET A POSITIVE RESULT, WE COULD STILL BE IN TIME TO DO SOMETHING ABOUT IT.
PLEASE BE HERE TOMORROW MORNING AT 9 O'CLOCK.
THIS CAN'T BE TRUE.
IT'S NOT TRUE! GIVE HIM BACK TO ME!!
ARE YOU LISTENING, MISS WILDFANG?

"FAUST WILDFANG'S (FUTURE!) TRAVEL JOURNAL."
WHAT...?

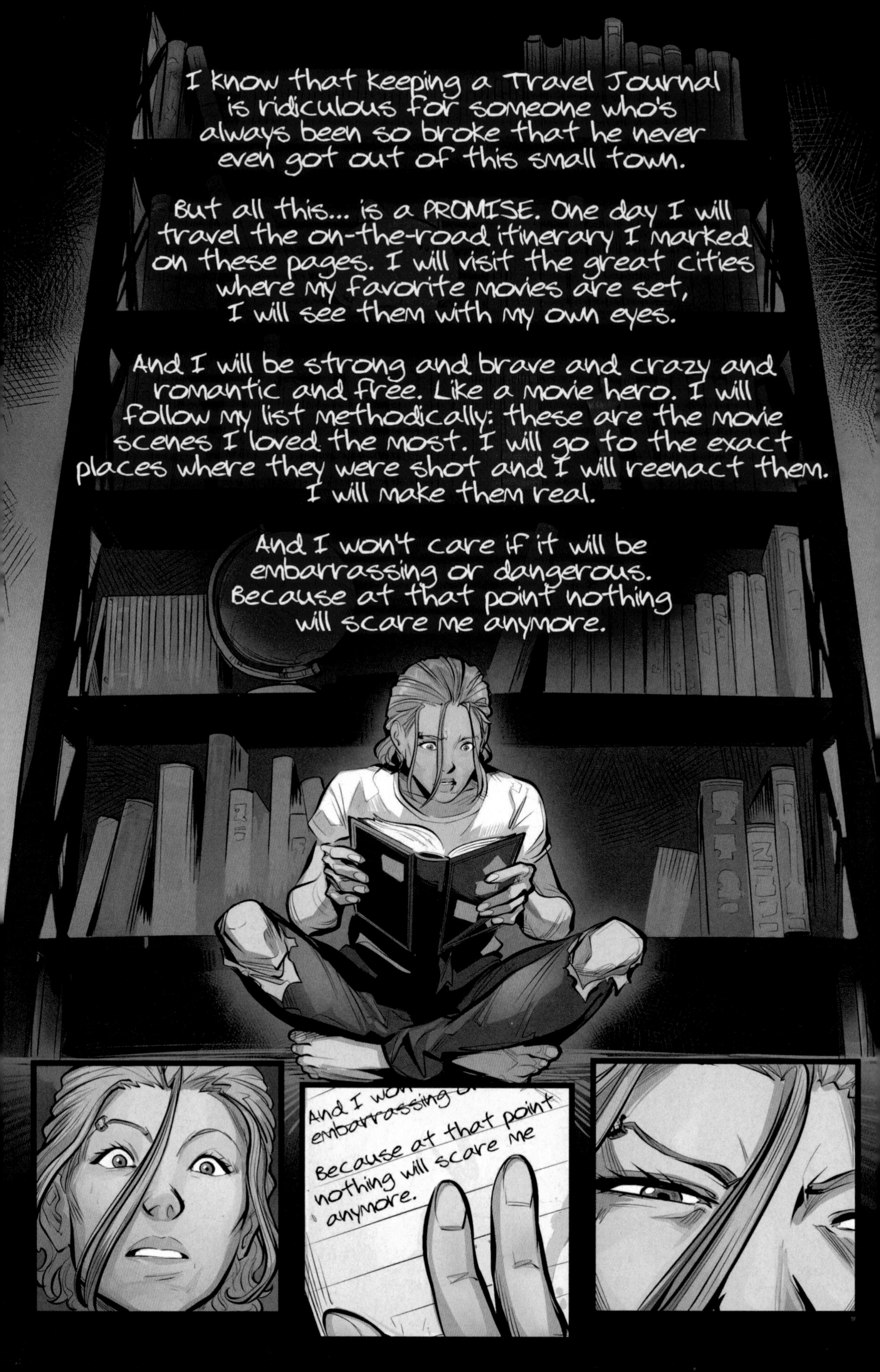
I know that keeping a Travel Journal is ridiculous for someone who's always been so broke that he never even got out of this small town.
But all this... is a PROMISE. One day I will travel the on-the-road itinerary I marked on these pages. I will visit the great cities where my favorite movies are set, I will see them with my own eyes.
And I will be strong and brave and crazy and romantic and free. Like a movie hero. I will follow my list methodically: these are the movie scenes I loved the most. I will go to the exact places where they were shot and I will reenact them. I will make them real.
And I won't care if it will be embarrassing or dangerous. Because at that point nothing will scare me anymore.
Because at that point nothing will scare me anymore.

ENOUGH TO PAY FOR THE FIRST TRAIN, AT LEAST...
CRASH
I'M DORIAN WILDFANG. AND NOTHING WILL SCARE ME ANYMORE.
SLAM!

BRAUEREI
BRAUEREI
FIRST STOP : ROME
I HOPE THERE'S A NIGHT TRAIN TO ITALY, EVEN THOUGH IT'S SATURDAY NIGHT...
Bahnhof

UHM?

SOOO... THIS MUST BE DESTINY WISHING ME GOOD LUCK.
AND THE DOOR IS NOT EVEN LOCKED...

FLIP
FLIP
OK. LET THE ADVENTURE BEGIN!

LET THE ADVENTURE BEGIN, DOC!
GOD... ARE YOU ALWAYS SO LOUD?
MMH-- NO ONE EVER MADE ME NOTICE, BUT I SUPPOSE I AM!
IS THE PAINKILLER DOING ITS JOB? DO YOU FEEL BETTER NOW?
YES, MUCH BETTER, THANK YOU...
I'M STILL PINCHING MYSELF TO TRY TO WAKE UP FROM THIS SURREAL SITUATION, THOUGH.
AND IS THAT WORKING, DOC?
NOT AT ALL. AND IT GETS WORSE EVERY TIME YOU CALL ME "DOC."
HAHAHA
TRAVELING THROUGH EUROPE TO REENACT MOVIE SCENES IN THE CITIES WHERE THEY WERE SHOT?
WHERE WOULD YOU GET AN IDEA LIKE THAT??
AND BESIDES, NORMAL PEOPLE DON'T STEAL A CAR WHEN THEY WANT TO GO ON A ROAD TRIP!
I'M SORRY IF I HAVE GIVEN YOU THE WRONG IMPRESSION, BUT I'M NOT BY ANY MEANS "NORMAL PEOPLE."
BESIDES, I NEVER OWNED A CAR. AND, WELL, I NEEDED ONE.

GOD... WELL, AT LEAST YOU ARE NOT A SERIAL KILLER.
WELL, AT LEAST I DON'T THINK YOU ARE. I MEAN, YOU WOULD HAVE ALREADY KILLED ME...?
COULD HAVE.
YOU KNOW, NORMAL PEOPLE DON'T SLEEP IN AN OPEN CAR, LEAVING THE KEYS WHERE EVERYONE CAN SEE THEM. AND WITHOUT A PHONE! YOU COULD HAVE FOUND YOURSELF IN STRANGE SITUATIONS!
THIS IS A STRANGE SITUATION, I'VE BEEN KIDNAPPED!!
NAAH. YOU'VE BEEN CHOSEN AS CO-DRIVER FOR AN AWESOME TRIP!
CO-DRIVER OF MY OWN CAR?
I HAVE ALREADY TOLD YOU, BIZARRE HANGOVER HALLUCINATION. TAKE US TO THE FIRST RAILWAY STATION SO I CAN RECOVER AND DRIVE BACK HOME AND YOU CAN GET ON A TRAIN AND GO ON WITH YOUR RECKLESS MISSION.
BELIEVE ME, I ALREADY HAVE BIGGER PROBLEMS TO SOLVE BACK HOME. I CAN'T HANDLE YOU, TOO.
MILANO
FIRENZE
MY NAME'S DORIAN, ANYWAY. AND I'M PRETTY SURE THAT THE FACT THAT YOU DIDN'T THROW ME OUT OF THE CAR RIGHT AWAY MEANS YOU DON'T DISLIKE THIS "HALLUCINATION" AS MUCH AS YOU SAY, DOC.
I'M JUST TOO WELL-MANNERED! NOW BE QUIET AND DRIVE!
AND MY NAME IS MAG!

WOW... IT'S HOT!
THIS SEEMS SUCH A NICE PLACE... EVER BEEN TO ITALY BEFORE, DOC?
(HOW TALL ARE YOU?!)
N-NO... NO. LET'S SAY I'VE NEVER HAD MUCH TIME TO TRAVEL IN MY LIFE.
Bologna Centrale Stazione
ME NEITHER... ALSO, I'VE ALWAYS BEEN BROKE, SO...
I AM BROKE, ACTUALLY.
DOESN'T SOUND LIKE THE BEST STARTING POINT FOR YOUR ADVENTURE.

THERE ARE SOME THINGS YOU MUST DO.
LIFE IS **FLEETING**, YOU KNOW?
ONE MOMENT YOU BELIEVE AT SOME POINT **THE WHOLE WORLD** WILL BE AT YOUR FINGERTIPS... WHEN YOU'LL BE READY, **ONE DAY**, EVERY PIECE OF THE PUZZLE WILL PERFECTLY FALL IN ITS PLACE.
THE NEXT MINUTE IT'S **ALL OVER**, DOC.

FLIP
SO, IF THERE'S SOMETHING YOU'D LIKE TO TRY, YOU SHOULD JUST DO IT.

THANKS FOR **THE LECTURE**, WEIRDO. BUT PEOPLE **DON'T** JUST SUDDENLY LEAVE FOR A LONG TRIP WITH THE FIRST PERSON WHO STEALS THEIR CAR.
WHY NOT? IT SOUNDS LIKE **THE BEGINNING OF A GREAT STORY**!

NO, NOT TO ME, NO... I'M JUST NOT THAT KIND OF PERSON.

AND JUDGING BY THE WAY THOSE STUDENTS ARE EYEING YOU, I THINK YOU WILL **NOT STRUGGLE** TO FIND ANOTHER "**COMPANION.**"
MH?

GUTEN MORGEN!
AHHH

YOU MAY BE RIGHT. BUT I DON'T WANT JUST ANY CO-PILOT!
YOU DON'T EVEN KNOW ME!
LET'S FIX THIS THEN!
YOU MIGHT FIND OUT YOU'RE JUST "THAT KIND OF PERSON"!

I... ENJOY YOUR ADVENTURE, DORIAN.

SIGH
I SEE... HAVE A NICE TRIP HOME, DOC.

THANKS FOR BEING "TOO WELL-MANNERED" TO ME.
(AND REMEMBER, EASY ON THE WILD BINGES!)

I AM DOCTOR MAGDALENE TRÄUMER, CURRENTLY WORKING ON PROJECT "WHAT THE FUCK IS HAPPENING TO ME." I AM IN NEED OF A FAST EVALUATION OF THE REVISED DATA TO PROVIDE AN EFFICIENT SOLUTION.
FLEETING
??
START EVALUATION: A- THIS STRING OF UNLIKELY COINCIDENCES IS FASCINATING. COULD TESTING WHERE A VERY ILL-ADVISED DECISION WOULD TAKE ME BE CONSIDERED A SCIENTIFIC EXPERIMENT?
B- MY PROFESSIONAL ETHICS ACTUALLY FORBID ME TO ABANDON AN INDIVIDUAL WHO HAS FALLEN IN AN EVIDENT STATE OF IRRESPONSIBILITY. AND SAID INDIVIDUAL LOOKS AS BROKE AS IT IS DETERMINED TO ACCOMPLISH ITS MISSION ALONE ANYWAY. ON THE OTHER HAND, IN MY CURRENT STATE THIS SEEMS POTENTIALLY THE MOST INTERESTING OCCASION TO SPEND THE PAYCHECKS OF A LIFETIME, WHICH I NEVER HAD CHANCE OR REASON TO TOUCH.
C- I HAVE BEEN, IT SEEMS, RECENTLY INFORMED THAT LIFE IS "FLEETING," AND I AM NOT POSITIVE THAT I WANT TO DIE WITHOUT KNOWING IF THERE IS SOMETHING OTHER THAN MY JOB THAT I MIGHT BE GOOD AT. IN ADDITION, IT IS VERY WARM HERE. AND MY FLAT IS COLD.
D- MOST RELEVANT DATA: KEEPING IN MIND THE RECENT CIRCUMSTANCES... AND HERE I WILL NEED TO GATHER ALL OF MY INTELLECTUAL HONESTY... DO I REALLY HAVE SOMETHING THAT I WANT TO GO BACK TO?

DORIAN! WAIT!

SO... IS THIS THE FAMOUS MOVIE SCENES TRAVEL JOURNAL?

EXACTLY. BUT DON'T LEAF THROUGH IT. I DON'T WANT ANY SPOILERS!

SPOILERS?? DIDN'T YOU WRITE THIS??
OH MY GOD. ARE WE GOING TO FOLLOW A LIST WITHOUT EVEN KNOWING WHERE IT WILL GET US?
THAT'S RIGHT. ISN'T IT AWESOME?

YOU HAVE MY WORD: WHATEVER HAPPENS, IT'S GONNA BE FUN.
SIGH
WHAT KIND OF WOMAN OF SCIENCE WOULD I BE IF I WERE TO SO HASTILY CHANGE MY DECISION?

BUT I'M WARNING YOU: I DON'T KNOW WHAT KIND OF SCENES YOU INTEND TO REENACT AND IF I WILL TAKE ANY PART IN THEM.
BESIDES, I TELL YOU, I AM BY NO MEANS THE ADVENTUROUS TYPE.
YOU ALREADY TOLD ME THAT MORE THAN ONCE AND I'VE ONLY MET YOU THIS MORNING, DOC.

SO... HOW ARE YOU GOING TO DO THIS?
DON'T YOU WANT TO AT LEAST GIVE THE ENDING A PEEK? JUST SO YOU KNOW HOW LONG IT WILL TAKE TO GET THERE, OR WHAT IS THE FINAL STOP...
NO... I HAVE FAITH IN THIS. I PREFER TO DO IT THIS WAY.

I DON'T SUPPOSE YOU WANT TO TELL ME WHO IS THE PERSON YOU TRUST SO MUCH.
NO, I'D RATHER NOT...
OKAY. THEN... I WILL TAKE YOU BOTH SIGHT UNSEEN.
HEY, I'M TAKING MY RISKS TOO, YOU KNOW? I DON'T EVEN KNOW WHAT KIND OF DOCTOR YOU ARE!
ONE OF THE GOOD ONES.
THAT'S ALL YOU NEED TO KNOW.
WHAT ABOUT ENJOYING THIS ADVENTURE WITHOUT HAVING TO ANSWER QUESTIONS WE DON'T WANT TO ANSWER?
IS THAT OKAY FOR YOU?
VERY WELL.
SO, IT'S A DEAL? NO TALKING ABOUT THE PAST?
THERE IS NO PAST.

ON OUR WAY NOW! THE ROAD TO ROME IS STILL PRETTY LONG!

ONE LAST THING...
YOU CAN BACK OUT WHENEVER YOU WANT. OKAY? NO JUDGMENT. THIS IS ALREADY A LOT FOR SOMEONE WHO'S "NOT THE ADVENTUROUS TYPE."

BUT AS FOR ME, I WILL SEE THIS THROUGH AT ALL COSTS.

OK...

...BUT I WILL DRIVE NOW!
ANY COMPLAINTS ABOUT MY DRIVING STYLE, DOC??
DO YOU WANT ME AND MY CAR OR DON'T YOU?

OK THEN, WE'LL TAKE TURNS!
LET'S TAKE TURNS, DOC!
ROMA
ROME

Issue #3 Cover A by ELISA ROMBOLI

Issue #3 Cover B by IOLANDA ZANFARDINO

THE BEST MOMENT TO GIVE UP ON SOMETHING IS RIGHT AFTER YOU'VE DECIDED TO DO IT. ISN'T IT? OTHERWISE YOU'LL END UP GETTING TOO INVOLVED WITH IT. IT WILL BECOME FAMILIAR.
TRAVELING WITH DORIAN BECAME FAMILIAR THE MOMENT I REALIZED THAT EVERYTHING ABOUT HER, FROM HER BRAZEN LAUGHTER TO THE WAY SHE COULD GET ON MY NERVES, THOUGH IT CLASHED WITH MY BEHAVIOR, IT ALSO SEEMED TO BE ITS NATURAL COUNTERPART.
BUT IT TOOK ME A WHILE TO LEARN HOW TO DEAL WITH IT.
NOW STAY QUIET!
C'MON DOC! MY CDS ARE IN THE TRUNK AND I'M DYING TO FIND OUT WHAT YOU KEEP IN THE STEREO!
OH - I NEVER WOULD HAVE THOUGHT YOU WERE THE NOSTALGIC ROCK TYPE!
I am a passenger And I ride, and I ride I ride through the city's backsides...
...I see the stars come out of the sky Yeah, they're bright in a hollow sky You know it looks so good tonight...
YOU SHOULDN'T JUDGE PEOPLE WHEN THEY ARE HANGOVER.
OR IN SHOCK. OR BOTH.
...I look through my window so bright I see the stars come out tonight
NOW I SEE IT! NOT BAD, MY CLOTHES LOOK GOOD ON YOU!
(A STUDDED BELT WOULD BE PERFECT NOW!)
DON'T RUB IT IN, PLEASE. AS SOON AS WE FIND AN OPEN SHOP I WILL DIVE IN IT.
I LOOK TEN YEARS YOUNGER... AND HONESTLY, I DON'T LIKE IT AT ALL.
I see the bright and hollow sky Over the city's ripped back sky And everything looks good tonight...

WELL, IF YOU'D RATHER STAY SMELLY... I WASN'T COMPLAINING ANYWAY!
OH, **BE QUIET**!
HAHAHA

Oh, come on, come on,
Come on, come on!
OOH--

And each time I tell myself that I
Well I think I've had enough.
But I'm gonna show you, baby
That a woman can be tough!

I want you to come on, come on...
C'MON! **SING WITH ME!** THIS IS YOUR CD!
EHM... NO, I'D RATHER NOT.

YOU MUST HAVE SUNG THIS A THOUSAND TIMES, **ADMIT IT**!
YES, BUT ALWAYS **ALONE**!
...come on, come on...

I AM A DOOOCTOOOR, I ONLY SING WHEN I AM **ALOOONE**!
And take it!
Take another little piece
of my heart now, baby!

Oh, oh, break it!
Break another little bit of my
heart now, darling, yeah, yeah!

SIGH
Oh, oh, have a--!
Have another little piece of my heart now, babe!
HEY, IF MY SINGING IS THIS BAD, I'LL STOP!
(DIDN'T MEAN TO TORTURE YOU...)
NO, YOU'RE NOT THAT BAD.
IT'S JUST... I USED TO SING THIS EVERY MORNING ON MY WAY TO WORK. IT WAS A GOOD WAY TO UNLOAD.
BUT I... DON'T WANT TO THINK ABOUT IT NOW.
WILL THEY MISS YOU, DOC?
I TOLD YOU, FEEL FREE TO USE MY PHONE TO CALL WHOEVER YOU WANT!
DIDN'T WE PROMISE JUST A COUPLE OF HOURS AGO NOT TO TALK ABOUT THE PAST?

AND KEEP YOUR EYES ON THE ROAD WHEN YOU DRIVE, YOU IRRESPONSIBLE WOMAN!
(SEE WHY I DON'T WANT YOU TO DRIVE??)
BELIEVE ME, I'VE DRIVEN SO MANY DIFFERENT VEHICLES FOR SO MANY DIFFERENT JOBS THAT I COULD DRIVE YOUR CAR WITH MY EYES SHUT!
LIKE THIS, SEE?
NO NO NO! DON'T YOU DARE!
OOKAY. BUT LOOK WHAT ELSE I CAN DO!
HAHAHA
OH MY GOD! PUT THAT GIRAFFE LEG BACK WHERE IT SHOULD BE!!
LISTEN, I'M REALLY GETTING MAD!
DORIAAAAAAN!
HAHAHAHA

ROME
WOW...
WE REALLY ARE IN ROME.
(AND I AM REALLY DRESSED LIKE THIS.)
HEY! THERE'S A LOT OF PEOPLE FOR BEING THIS LATE!
(IS EVERYTHING THIS HUGE HERE?)
WHERE ARE WE HEADED, PRECISELY?
I KNOW IT'S LATE... BUT I THINK IT'S THE PERFECT TIME FOR THE VERY FIRST MISSION ON OUR LIST.
THE PLACE IS JUST A WALK AWAY...

ARE YOU REALLY NOT GOING TO TELL ME ANYTHING UNTIL WE GET THERE?
AND IT'S GETTING REALLY LATE NOW!
OH... MY GOODNESS.
OR, AS I WOULD PHRASE IT, HOLY SHIT!

BUT-- WHAT DO WE HAVE TO DO NOW?
LET'S GO.
WHERE DO WE-- DORIAN?
I FEAR I KNOW WHAT MOVIE WE ARE TALKING ABOUT!

I REALLY DON'T THINK THIS IS PERMITTED!
YEAH, NEITHER DO I!
SPLASH
DOC... COME HERE!
HURRY UP!

NOT IN A MILLION YEARS!
I DON'T DO THINGS THAT ARE ILLEGAL!

OH, COME OOON! WHEN'S THIS GONNA HAPPEN AGAIN?

I-I DON'T...

HEY! WHAT ARE YOU DOING??
ROMA CAPITALE

OH SHIT.
RUN!!

STOP!! IT'S THE POLICE!

HAHAHAHA

FIRST MISSION ACCOMPLISHED, DOC!!
POLIZIA ROMA CAPITALE
POLIZIA ROMA CAPITALE
SHUT UUUUP!

PUNK'S NOT DEAD
I CAN'T BELIEVE THIS.
MY FIRST DAY ABROAD, AND I ALREADY RISKED BEING ARRESTED!
DOOOC!
I SWEAR THE SECOND MISSION ON THE LIST WILL BE LESS TRAUMATIC!
LOOK WHAT I RENTED!
TA-DAA
WE JUST HAVE TO TAKE A RIDE ON THIS!
OH... WHAT A VINTAGE, NICE THING!
AND YOU KNOW HOW TO RIDE IT?
I TOLD YOU, I CAN DRIVE ANYTHING! COME ON, JUMP IN!

WOOH!
VROOOM
HOLD ON TIGHT DOC! ENJOY THE RIDE!
VROOOOM

IT'S... INCREDIBLE.

IT'S ALL SO THRILLING. I **CAN'T BELIEVE** I'M HERE!
TRUE. WE SHOULD TAKE PICTURES!

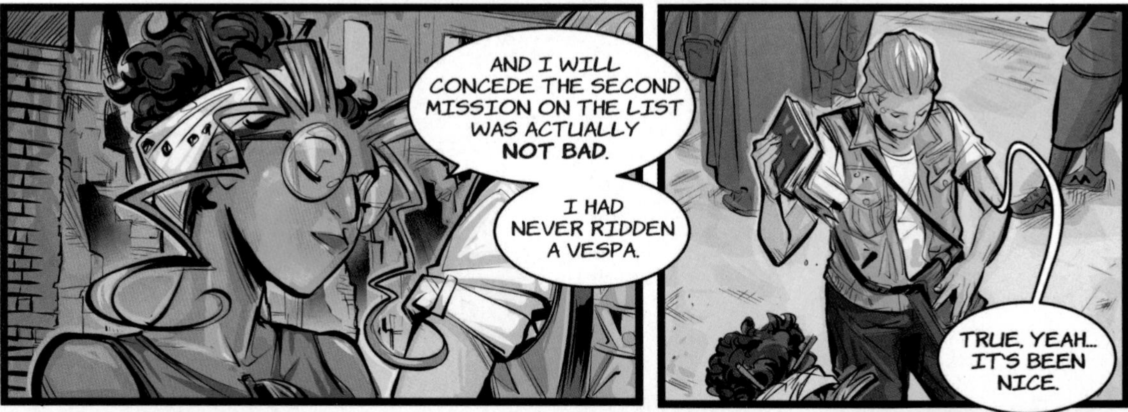
AND I WILL CONCEDE THE SECOND MISSION ON THE LIST WAS ACTUALLY **NOT BAD**.
I HAD NEVER RIDDEN A VESPA.
TRUE, YEAH... IT'S BEEN NICE.

YOU KNOW... WHEN YOU DON'T DO ANYTHING **RIDICULOUS OR EMBARRASSING**, IT'S ALMOST PLEASANT TO SPEND TIME WITH--

COFF COFF

INHA—LING
WHA-- ?

MY NAME IS MAXIMUS DECIMUS MERIDIUS.

NONONO DORIAN!
(LIKE THIS, WHEN I LEAST EXPECT IT??)

COMMANDER OF THE ARMIES OF THE NORTH, GENERAL OF THE FELIX LEGIONS AND LOYAL SERVANT TO THE TRUE EMPEROR, MARCUS AURELIUS.
WILL YOU AT LEAST **LOWER YOUR VOICE**! EVERYBODY'S **WATCHING US**!!

FATHER TO A MURDERED SON. HUSBAND TO A MURDERED WIFE.

AND I WILL HAVE MY VENGEANCE, IN THIS LIFE OR THE NEXT.

WAAAH

THANKS, PEOPLE! GRAZIE!

OK, YOU DID IT. LET'S GO NOW. LET'S GO!
NO MORE SIGHTSEEING FOR TODAY!

HEY! DONE ALREADY?
WHAT. YOU THOUGHT I WOULD TAKE LONG?
I KNOW WHAT I WEAR. I JUST NEED TO GET IN. ASK. GET OUT.
UHMM... IS THIS IT?
WHAT?

THESE CLOTHES ARE SO DULL AND... SAD.
(HOW DID YOU MANAGE TO FIND ALL THIS GREY STUFF IN A STREET THAT IS SO FULL OF COLORFUL WINDOWS??)
PRECISELY. I KNOW WHAT I WEAR. I DON'T NEED ANYTHING ELSE.
NO, NO. COME ON DOC! WE NEED APPROPRIATE OUTFITS FOR THIS ADVENTURE!
LET'S GO, I'LL GO IN WITH YOU!
DORIAN, NOO-- I'M OK WITH THOSE!
YOU WERE OK UNTIL NOW! THIS IS THE NEW "EUROPE TOUR DOCTOR"!
LET'S GO CHOOSE SOMETHING FUN, SOMETHING COLORFUL!
AAAALRIGHT... BUT I WANT TO KEEP THOSE ANYWAY!
SOUNDS FAIR.
BUT COME ALONG NOW, I'LL BE YOUR PERSONAL SHOPPER!
AH! I'M IN GOOD HANDS THEN--

MY GOD! IT'S TRUE, THEN, THAT GREAT MINDS LOVE CHAOS! THIS TRUNK DOESN'T MAKE ANY SENSE!
HEY, HAD I KNOWN THAT I WAS LEAVING FOR A ROAD TRIP, I WOULD HAVE TIDIED IT UP!
(OR I WOULDN'T HAVE. NO, I THINK NOT.)
SO WE ARE THROUGH WITH THE ROMAN MISSIONS? REALLY? OR AM I IN FOR SOME OTHER SURPRISE?
WE REALLY ARE, NO MORE MISSIONS ON THE LIST.
WE LEAVE FOR SPAIN TOMORROW!
THAT IS, IF THERE WILL BE ANY ROOM LEFT FOR SLEEPING IN THE CAR AFTER WE'VE SQUEEZED IN YOUR NEW PURCHASES!
MMMM... I ADMIT I QUITE LIKE THIS NEW STYLE. MAYBE I SHOULD THANK YOUR STUBBORNNESS FOR ONCE.
YOU LOOK AMAZING, DOC!
AND IF IN MADRID YOU'LL STOP CARING ABOUT WHAT PEOPLE THINK AND START SERIOUSLY PARTICIPATING IN THE MISSIONS, IT WILL MAKE YOU IRRESISTIBLE!

OH WELL... "IRRESISTIBLE" REALLY DOESN'T SOUND LIKE ME.
AND AS FOR "NOT CARING ABOUT PEOPLE"... IT IS DEFINITELY NOT MY LIFE PHILOSOPHY. **NOT AT ALL**.

MH?

HEY, DOC... EHM. I THINK THESE ARE **IMPORTANT**, YOU KNOW. YOU MIGHT WANT TO SAVE THEM FROM THIS CHAOS...
COUGH!
AH.
PAPERS TO SIGN
VERY URGENT

RIIIIP
SO, YES... GOOD THING WE DECIDED NOT TO ASK EACH OTHER QUESTIONS.
OTHERWISE I DEFINITELY WOULD HAVE ASKED YOU OF THAT TIME YOU **TORE UP** SOME DIVORCE PAPERS.
YOU KNOW, LESS THAN A MINUTE AGO?
YEAH, RIGHT. **TOO BAD** WE PROMISED.

WOW--
SIGH
SORRY, I MIGHT HAVE OVERREACTED...
I SUPPOSE IT DOESN'T MAKE ANY DIFFERENCE IF I TELL YOU ABOUT IT. IT'S JUST THAT... IT'S NOT A GREAT STORY.
A FEW YEARS AGO I MARRIED A PHD COLLEAGUE AND... NOTHING, REALLY. I GOT SOME RESEARCH FUNDS FOR A PROJECT I CARED DEEPLY ABOUT, SOMETHING I FELT WAS JUST RIGHT. HE INSTEAD CHOSE AN EASIER, MORE INDIVIDUALISTIC PATH, INSIDE THE SAME COMPANY.
I WAS VERY TAKEN... WITH MY RESEARCH, NOT MY MARRIAGE.
THINGS DIDN'T WORK OUT.
AND NOW I KEEP FINDING COPIES OF THOSE DOCUMENTS EVERYWHERE.
THE END. NOW LET'S TRY TO FIND SOME ROOM FOR THESE NEW BLANKETS, SHALL WE...
OH-- YES.
THANKS FOR THE BLANKETS, "DOCTOR CHARITY"!
AND SO, DESPITE MY PAINFUL CONFUSION, DESPITE THE ROARING STORM INSIDE...
AND DESPITE THE FACT THAT, FROM THE MOMENT WE MET, "DOCTOR MORALISM" NEVER STOPPED SCOLDING ME...

I FOUND MYSELF SERIOUSLY TAKING NOTICE THAT, ANYWAY, SHE IS SINGLE. STRAIGHT, THOUGH, APPARENTLY.
SAME OLD STORY, THEN...
(WAIT, WHAT IF SHE IS BISEXUAL?)
IN ANY CASE, IT IS NOT SOMETHING I CAN DEAL WITH NOW, IN MY CONDITION.
FORGIVE ME, FAUST.

I KNOW I SAID I WOULDN'T PEEK, BUT I NEED TO UNDERSTAND WHERE YOU WANT TO TAKE ME
WHERE YOU WANT ME TO GET TO...
Germany
...HOME?
Now, come back home and do something TRUE. Something that will make reality better than any movie
many
WHAT??

ARE YOU MAKING FUN OF ME, FAUST?
THIS SOUNDS A BIT COMPLICATED, YOU KNOW! YOU'RE NOT MAKING THIS EASY FOR ME IN ANY WAY!
SOMETHING TRUE? WHAT DOES TRUTH MEAN FOR SOMEONE LIKE YOU?

I SHOULD HAVE SEEN SUCH AN IDEALISTIC FINALE COMING FROM YOU.
ARE YOU TELLING ME THAT I WILL DO ALL THIS AND I WON'T BE ABLE TO COMPLETE YOUR LIST AT THE LAST MISSION?
SIGH

YOU'LL DRIVE ME CRAZY, FAUST...
GOD. I MISS YOU SO MUCH.

Issue #4 Cover A by ELISA ROMBOLI

Issue #4 Cover B art by IOLANDA ZANFARDINO

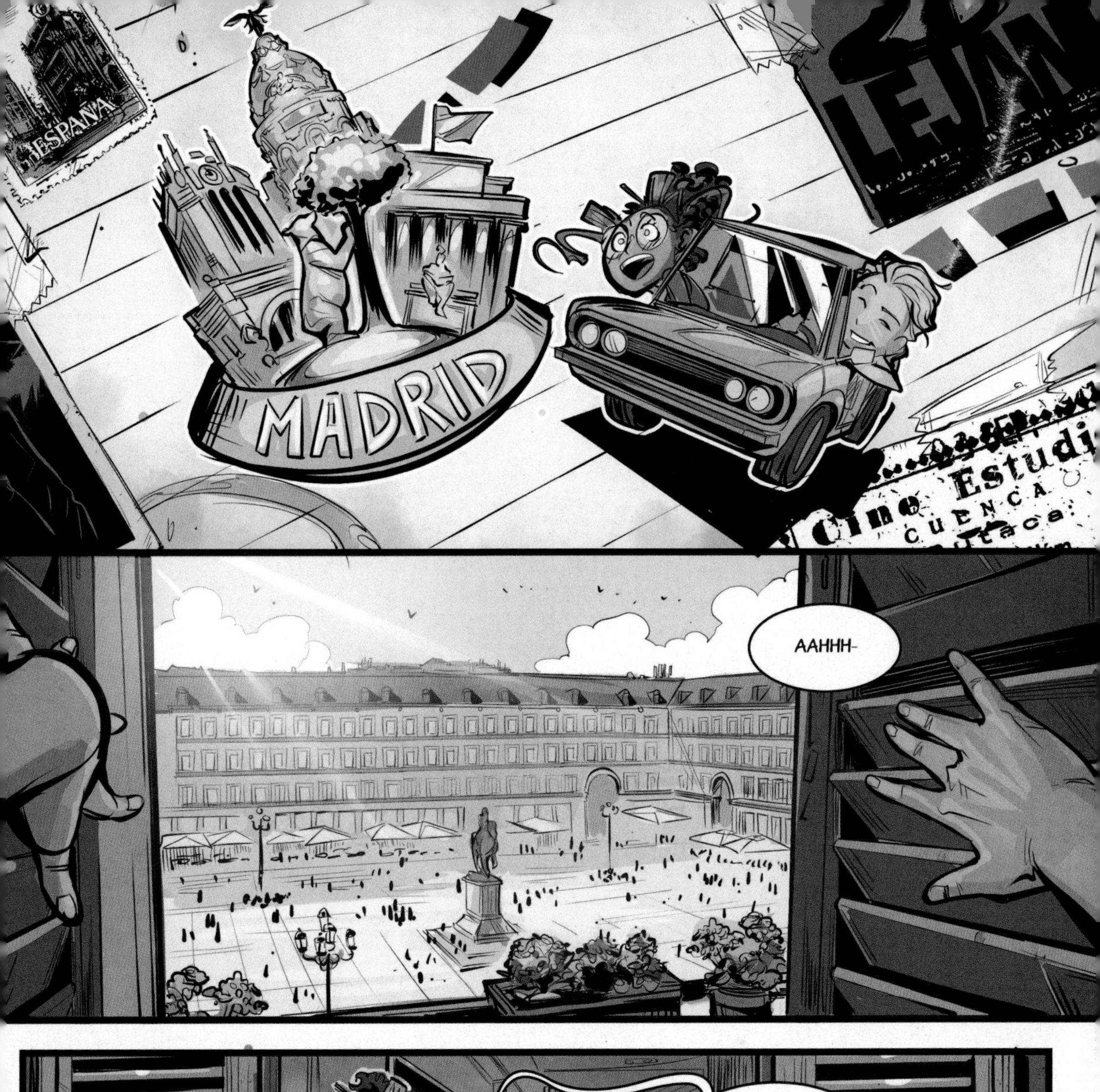
ESPAÑA
MADRID
Cine Estudi
CUENCA
AAHHH-

I OFFICIALLY CONFIRM I HAVE BECOME TOO OLD TO SLEEP IN A CAR.
ONE MORE NIGHT AND MY BACK WOULD HAVE MUTINIED.

WHOA-- THIS IS A LUXURY ROOM, DOC!

I WOULD SAY IT IS PRETTY AVERAGE... YOU SHOULD SEE THE HOTELS THEY SEND ME TO WHEN I HAVE TO **SPEAK AT CONFERENCES**.
(AND EVEN THEN, IT IS NOT SOMETHING TO GET TOO EXCITED ABOUT.)
THIS IS SOOO COOL! I'D NEVER BEEN IN **AN HOTEL**!
REALLY? NEVER?
WHEN I WAS IN HIGH SCHOOL I'D OFTEN TAKE A TRAIN TO GO SEE THIS GIRL WHO WAS **MY SWEETHEART** AT THE TIME...
I OBVIOUSLY COULDN'T SLEEP WITH HER AT HER PARENTS' HOUSE, SO I USED TO SPEND THE NIGHTS IN THE CHEAPEST HOSTELS I COULD FIND. YOU KNOW, THE ONES WITH HUGE DORMITORIES...
I'M SURPRISED THEY WOULDN'T ALLOW SUCH A **GOOD, EVEN-TEMPERED MATCH** NEAR THEIR DAUGHTER!

HEY. I WAS A LOT MORE SERIOUS WHEN I WAS YOUNGER, ACTUALLY.
ALSO, I AM A **REAL HARD WORKER**! A MORE THAN RESPECTABLE MATCH!
AND WITH SUCH A **BEAUTIFUL FACE**, TOO! DON'T YOU THINK? I MEAN, LOOK AT THESE **CHEEKBONES**!
OH, **SHUT UP**!
SOFT
OH MY GOD, THOSE PILLOWS ARE SO SOOOOFT!
AND LOOK!! MY FEET **ALMOST FIT IN**!! AT THE HOSTEL THEY WOULD ALWAYS STICK OUT OF THE BED!

NOW I'LL GO TAKE A VEEEERY LONG SHOWER!
ANOTHER AWESOME FEATURE OF THIS ROOM! THANKS, **SUGAR DOC**!
Y-YES, UHM, DON'T WORRY...

I KNOW, THIS WAS SUCH A CLICHE. BUT I SWEAR IN THAT MOMENT I STILL WOULDN'T HAVE BEEN ABLE TO SAY WHAT **WAS ABOUT TO HAPPEN**...

MY HEAD WAS SO FULL WITH OTHER THINGS I JUST DIDN'T HAVE THE STRENGTH TO ENTERTAIN ANOTHER THOUGHT.
ALL I COULD DO WAS LET MYSELF GO WITH THE FLOW OF OUR MISSIONS...
MADRID
Make banknotes rain over Madrid and let the crowd go crazy
THIS ONE IS HARD...
HOW ARE WE GONNA PULL THIS OF?
(I MEAN, WE DO HAVE FUNDS BUT CERTAINLY NOT ENOUGH...)
MMMMH... I'LL THINK OF SOMETHING, DON'T WORRY.
OH, THANKS!
WHY, THIS IS WONDERFUL!
I WAS SO HUNGRY!
COFF COFF
SO-- WELL. IT'S HARD TO CHAT IF WE CAN'T ASK EACH OTHER QUESTIONS...
TRULY. I'M GOOD AT FIRST DATE CHITCHATS, BUT THIS ONE IS DIFFICULTY LEVEL A+!
AND IT'S NOT EVEN A DATE.
OF COURSE, I KNOW!
UHMMM... LET'S REVIEW WHAT I ALREADY KNOW ABOUT YOU.

IT SEEMS YOUR NAME IS MAG. YOU REPEAT THAT QUITE OFTEN.
AND YOU KEEP IGNORING IT ANYWAY.
YOU ARE SOME KIND OF DOCTOR, I THINK. YOU LIKE NOSTALGIC ROCK, BUT WON'T LET ME HEAR HOW YOU SING IT AND YOU DIDN'T THINK YOU WOULD LOOK GOOD IN NICE CLOTHES. BUT YOU DO.
SEE? YOU ALREADY KNOW A LOT OF THINGS!
PFF
WOW, DID I JUST MAKE YOU LAUGH? I'M DEFINITELY DOING BETTER THAN IN REAL DATES!
HAHAHA
DO YOU SEE, DARLING? SHEER MADNESS.
WHAT A SHAME. RIGHT HERE IN THE SQUARE WHERE EVERYONE CAN SEE THEM.
SINCE THEY HAD THEIR "MARRIAGES" APPROVED THEY THINK THEY CAN DO WHATEVER THEY WANT. AND IN FRONT OF THE KIDS, TOO!
AND DID YOU NOTICE THE WAITER? THESE PEOPLE ARE EVERYWHERE!
RESTAU
THANK YOU!
!!

OOOOPS!
I AM EVER SO SORRY, GOOD FELLOW!
FRUSHHH

DOC. RUN!
OH NO. NOT AGAIN.
(I AM A WOMAN OF SCIENCE! I AM NOT MADE TO RUN!!)
WHAT... COME BACK HERE YOU FILTHY--
I'M SORRY, SIR, BUT YOU STILL NEED TO PAY THE BILL! YOU CAN'T GO AWAY LIKE THIS.
DIDN'T YOU SEE WHAT HAPPENED? HOW DO YOU PRESUME I CAN--
I DON'T KNOW WHAT YOU'RE TALKING ABOUT, SIR, BUT HERE YOU CAN'T DECIDE TO "DO WHATEVER YOU WANT" AND JUST WALK AWAY WITHOUT PAYING.
(AND IN FRONT OF THE KIDS, TOO!)
I WILL CONCEDE THAT WAS AN EXCELLENT INTUITION... BUT YOU DON'T DO THESE THINGS!
OK?
OH COME ON, DOC, YOU'RE LAUGHING TOO!
HAHAHAHA
I EMPHATICALLY DENY IT! ABSOLUTELY!
AND NOW YOU MUST STOP FAKING YOU DON'T KNOW THAT MY NAME IS MAG!

BAM BAM BAM
MAG! MAAAG!
BAM BAM BAM
DON'T YOU DARE IGNORE ME IN PERSON, TOO!
BLOCKING MY NUMBER WAS VERY CHILDISH OF YOU! ENOUGH NOW!
MAAAG!
DOCTOR HIKMET, WE DON'T PAY YOU TO SPEND YOUR DAY KNOCKING ON AN EMPTY LAB'S DOOR.

I-I'M JUST LOOKING FOR DOCTOR TRÄUMER.

THEN YOU MIGHT HAVE TO KNOCK FOREVER. DOCTOR TRÄUMER RESIGNED THREE DAYS AGO.

WHAT?... THAT'S IMPOSSIBLE.

BZZZZ
GO BACK TO WORK, DOCTOR HIKMET. DON'T MAKE ME ASK AGAIN.
BZZZZ
MAG WOULD **NEVER** DO THIS.
BZZZZ
AND HER PHONE HAS BEEN **OFF FOR THREE DAYS**...
WHAT IS GOING ON HERE?...

NO, OK, I THINK WE NEED TO RECONSIDER WHO SHOULD CARRY OUT THIS SECOND SPANISH MISSION.
DON'T YOU EVEN THINK ABOUT IT. THIS ONE IS PERFECT JUST LIKE THIS.
WHEN WILL I EVER GET THE CHANCE AGAIN TO SEE YOU AND NOT ME GETTING EMBARRASSED?
I'LL BE AWFUL! I'LL FALL FROM THE HEELS. I'LL FALL!
STOP WHINING. DON'T MAKE ME DO THE BAD DOCTOR.
Welcome to our "Amateur Night"! Our team of professionals will make your secret dream come true for one night!
NOCHE AMATEUR! DRAG QUEEN SHOW
THIS WAY, AMATEURS!
GOOD EVENING, GIRLS! CAN I COMMISSION A WORK?
WOULD YOU PLEASE HELP MY FRIEND SHOW HER HIDDEN POTENTIAL JUST FOR TONIGHT?
OOH- AN ASPIRING FAUX QUEEN?
WELL, AT LEAST SHE WON'T NEED TUCKING...
PSST PSST
YEAH, THAT'S NICE, BUT HAVE YOU SEEN HOW MUCH WORK WILL BE NEEDED HERE?

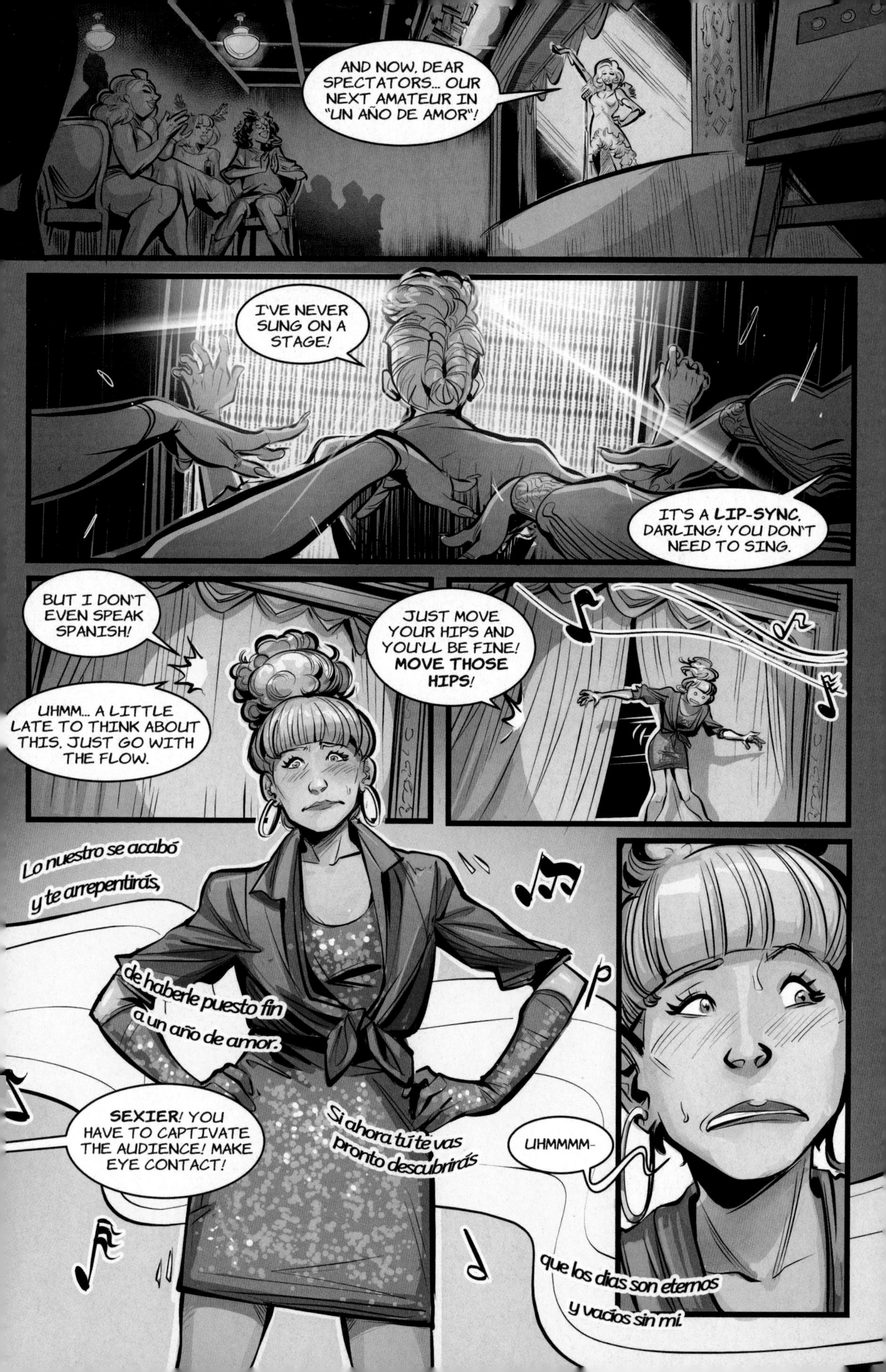
AND NOW, DEAR SPECTATORS... OUR NEXT AMATEUR IN "UN AÑO DE AMOR"!
I'VE NEVER SUNG ON A STAGE!
IT'S A LIP-SYNC, DARLING! YOU DON'T NEED TO SING.
BUT I DON'T EVEN SPEAK SPANISH!
UHMM... A LITTLE LATE TO THINK ABOUT THIS. JUST GO WITH THE FLOW.
JUST MOVE YOUR HIPS AND YOU'LL BE FINE! MOVE THOSE HIPS!
Lo nuestro se acabó
y te arrepentirás,
de haberle puesto fin
a un año de amor.
SEXIER! YOU HAVE TO CAPTIVATE THE AUDIENCE! MAKE EYE CONTACT!
Si ahora tú te vas
pronto descubrirás
UHMMMM-
que los dias son eternos
y vacíos sin mí.

WOOOHOOOOO! BRAVOOO!
Recordarás nuestros días felices
recordarás el sabor de mis besos
Y entenderás en un solo momento
que significa un año de amor.
BRAVOooo

FRANCE
SPAIN
I STILL CAN'T BELIEVE WHAT YOU MADE ME DO, DOC.
HEY, IT WAS **A MISSION**! I WAS JUST BEING DUTIFUL! YOU SHOULD BE PROUD OF ME!
AND LOOK, YOU WERE **NOT BAD** AT ALL...
THAT WAS HORRIBLE, PLEASE, LET'S STOP TALKING ABOUT IT!

Busted flat in Baton Rouge, waitin' for a train
When I's feelin' near as faded as my jeans

Windshield wipers slappin' time
MMMHH...
WHAT IF I ASKED YOU FOR SOMETHING YOU "**NEVER DO**" IN RETURN?...
I's holdin' Bobby's hand in mine
We sang every song that driver knew

LET ME GUESS...

SHALL WE SING, DOC?
DON'T GET USED TO IT.

* "ME AND BOBBY MCGEE"
COPYRIGHT BY KRIS KRISTOFFERSON AND FRED FOSTER.

STOP THE CAR!
WHOA! DORIAN??
WE CAN'T STOP HERE! DORIAN! GET BACK IN THE CAR!
I'LL BE RIGHT BACK, DOC!!
NO TRESSPASSING PRIVATE PROPERTY
YOU CAN'T GO THERE DORIAAAAN!
HAHAHA
~SIGH~

THERE YOU GO, DOC, YOU CAN BURY YOUR FACE IN IT!
JUST A **THANK YOU** FOR OUR SONG!

YOU'RE CRAZY! **YOU ARE CRAZY**, YOU KNOW THAT??

THAT STRONG SCENT INVADED THE CAR.
IT NEVER WENT AWAY COMPLETELY... UNTIL THE DAY IT GOT DESTROYED.

MISTER HIKMET...
YES!

I MUST CONFIRM THAT THE STATE THE APARTMENT WAS LEFT IN SEEMS TO INDICATE THAT THE PERSON LIVING HERE WAS PLANNING TO COME BACK **AND SHE DIDN'T**.
THIS COULD CONFIRM YOUR CONCERN THAT THE RESIDENT HAS **DISAPPEARED SUDDENLY**.
WE COULD NOT FIND ANY TRACES IN TOWN OF THE CAR WHOSE PLATE NUMBER YOU GAVE US. WE WILL WIDEN THE FIELD OF RESEARCH AND KEEP YOU INFORMED.

SEE YOU SOON, MISTER HIKMET. PLEASE STAY AVAILABLE.
OF COURSE. SEE YOU SOON, THANKS FOR THE HELP.

PLEASE, MAG, TELL ME YOU DIDN'T DO ANYTHING STUPID.
JUST PLEASE...

PARIS
AAAAH! THERE IT IS. THERE IT IS!
HERE WE ARE!
KEEP CALM, DOC! LET'S AT LEAST FIND A PARKING SPOT BEFORE YOU JUMP OUT!
EVERYTHING IS SO UNBELIEVABLE! LESS THAN A WEEK AGO I WAS SURE I KNEW HOW MY WHOLE LIFE WOULD HAVE GONE ON... AND NOW, INSTEAD, I'M IN PARIS!
AND I'VE BEEN TO ROME! MADRID!!
(AND LOOK!! DO YOU KNOW HOW LONG IT'S BEEN SINCE I LET MY HAIR DOWN IN PUBLIC??)

I'M STARTING TO ENJOY THIS, YOU KNOW? THIS DOING EVERYTHING I NEVER DID...
MAYBE I SHOULD JUST GIVE UP AND START ANEW...
GIVE UP... WHAT DO YOU MEAN?
AND THE SCENES WE'RE GOING TO RECREATE HERE MUST BE SO POETIC!
YEAH. THIS TIME I'M SURE IT'S GOING TO BE SOMETHING SOFT AND NOT ILLEGAL AT ALL!
COME ON DOC, YOU DIDN'T SAY A WORD!
IT COULD HAVE BEEN WORSE, YOU KNOW...

GOD... I'VE NEVER DONE SUCH... ACTS OF VANDALISM.
Le Monde est à Nous
I FIGURED. OUR TEEN YEARS MUST HAVE BEEN VERY DIFFERENT...
BUT YOU'RE NOT BAD AT ALL! YOU'VE DEFINITELY SWITCHED TO DOCTOR NOT-THINKING-TWICE!
I WAS JUST EXPECTING SOMETHING DIFFERENT.
DON'T WORRY, WE STILL HAVE THREE PARISIAN MISSIONS! I'M SURE SOME OF THEM WILL BE OF YOUR TASTE...
FSHHH
WELL, AT LEAST THIS TIME WE DON'T HAVE TO RUN AWAY.
HEY! STOP THERE, YOU LITTLE THUGS!
OH NO.

DOC, RUN!

I KNEW IT! THIS TIME THEY EVEN LOOK MEANER!!

STOP! IT'S THE POLICE!

STOP, STOP! I DON'T SEE THEM ANYMORE!
OH GOD, WE **FINALLY** LOST THEM! I ALMOST GAVE UP HOPE!
ANF ANF
... DOC?
... WE DID IT! WE **DID IT**!
WE WERE **AWESOME**! IT WAS **CRAZY**!!
WOOHOO! I'M STARTING TO LIKE THIS NOT-THINKING-TWICE THING!
REALLY, DOC? BUT THEN MAKING YOU DO IT WON'T BE FUN FOR ME ANYMORE!
COME ON, **COME ON**! WHAT'S THE NEXT THING ON THE LIST??

PARIS
Falling in love in front of the Moulin Rouge lights

UHM... WELL...

ROUGE
MOULIN ROUGE
SO? WHAT IS IT?
WELL... I THINK WE DID EVERYTHING FOR TODAY.

Issue #5 Cover A art by ELISA ROMBOLI

Issue #5 Cover B art by IOLANDA ZANFARDINO

DEFINITELY PLEASANT, TO BE IN A PLACE THAT IS SO OVERFLOWING WITH CULTURE.
INDEED. AND **OUR TRUE PURPOSE** IS NOT IMPAIRING OUR ELEGANCE IN ANY WAY.
I DO TOTALLY AGREE, **LADY DOC**.
BESIDES, I AM GLAD TO INFORM YOU THAT I ALREADY BOOKED OUR TICKETS FOR THE FERRY WE WILL EMBARK MY HUMBLE VEHICLE ON SO THAT WE CAN HEAD STRAIGHT TO **OUR NEXT STOP**.
SPLENDID! SUCH A PROVIDENT WOMAN.
AM I WRONG OR THIS IS THE RIGHT PLACE TO START OUR MISSION?
PLEASE, AFTER YOU, **SIR DORIAN**.
AAAAND... **TIMER SET**!

STOP!
IT'S FORBIDDEN TO RUN IN THE HALLS!
THE NINE MINUTE AND 45 SECOND RECORD – BROKEN!
WOOHOO! I WAS HOPING THAT ALL THE TRAINING WE'VE HAD WOULD PAY OFF!
MEIN GOTT! IF WE ARE TO KEEP GOING LIKE THIS I WILL HAVE TO STOP SMOKING!
STOP COMPLAINING. AT LEAST YOU AREN'T WEARING THESE INSTRUMENTS OF THE DEVIL!!
BEFORE WE GO TO LUNCH, I ABSOLUTELY NEED TO CHANGE.
HAHAHA

MMMHH! I LOVE FRENCH PASTRIES! CAN WE FILL THE WHOLE TRUNK WITH THEM? **PLEASE**?
TRY NOT TO GET AS CARRIED AWAY AS USUAL!
THOUGH I HAVE TO ADMIT IT MIGHT BE A NICE WAY TO CELEBRATE ALL OUR **SUCCESSFUL MISSIONS**!
SPEAKING OF WHICH... ISN'T THIS THE **PERFECT PLACE** FOR OUR NEXT MISSION ON THE LIST?
MMMH. WE CAN ESTABLISH THAT EASILY...
SO... HER?
MMMMM... WITH HIM?
SHALL WE SAY WITH **HER**?
PERFECT!
LET'S GO THEN! LIKE WE REHEARSED, DOC.

HEY! MAY I ASK FOR THE BIGGEST TAKEAWAY BOX OF... **EVERYTHING** YOU HAVE ON THE COUNTER?
HAHAHA- DON'T WORRY, I GOT YOU!

HELLO! SORRY TO BOTHER YOU... EHM...
OH... HAVE WE MET BEFORE?

SURE, IT MUST BE HARD TO FOCUS ON WORK WHEN YOU HAVE SUCH A PRETTY GIRL **THROWING GLANCES** AT YOU ALL DAY LONG!

NO, IT'S JUST THAT...
SEE, I'VE BEEN WONDERING IF THAT REALLY HOT GIRL BEHIND THE COUNTER WAS LOOKING AT ME... INSTEAD I REALIZED SHE'D BEEN **STARING AT YOU**!

WHAT? **HER**? THE GIRL WITH THE BOOK? **ARE YOU SERIOUS**?

T-THE BARTENDER, YOU MEAN? ARE YOU SURE? **LOOKING AT ME**?

I AM VERY SERIOUS! SHE'S BEEN LOOKING AT YOU AND SIGHING FOR A WHILE NOW! IF I WERE YOU, I WOULD **OFFER HER A MADELEINE**...
YOU THINK SO? SHOULD I?

YEAH, I WANTED TO INFORM YOU SO MAYBE YOU CAN TELL HER TO STOP... OR TO **KEEP GOING STRONGER**.
UHMM... YEAH, RIGHT, THANKS FOR THE WARNING! I-I'LL THINK ABOUT IT.

I CAN'T BELIEVE IT'S WORKING!
DORIAN, LOOK!
WE ACTUALLY STARTED A "LOVE AT FIRST SIGHT"!
WHAT IF SOMEONE SOMEDAY MADE HER NOTICE THE WAY I LOOK AT HER...?
GOD, DORIAN, YOU'RE AN IDIOT.
I CAN'T BE SUCH A COWARD. I PUSHED HER TO BEGIN THIS JOURNEY, NOW I HAVE TO TELL HERE HOW IT ENDS.
SHE MUST KNOW EVERYTHING. I MUST TELL HER.
EXCUSE ME, LADIES, YOUR TAKEAWAY BOX IS READY!
OH! YES, I'M COMING TO PAY AT THE REGISTER!

I'LL BE RIGHT BACK!
AND THE SCOLDING ABOUT THE UNDOUBTEDLY DISPROPORTIONATE AMOUNT OF PASTRIES YOU'VE BOUGHT IS ONLY POSTPONED.
IT'S UNBELIEVABLE... WHEN IT WAS ONLY ABOUT ME IT WASN'T AS SUFFOCATING A THOUGHT AS IT IS NOW THAT I THINK IT MIGHT HURT HER.
I CAN'T RISK HER RECIPROCATING MY FEELINGS ONLY TO FIND OUT I'M NOT WORTH THE TROUBLE.
ONLY TO...
ONLY TO FIND HERSELF IN AN HOSPITAL ROOM, SOONER THAN LATER, TO TAKE BACK HOME MY FEW THINGS.

I WANTED TO THANK YOU FOR PUSHING ME, THAT DAY AT THE STATION.
I KNOW YOU MUST HAVE THOUGHT I WOULD GIVE UP SOON... BUT NOW I'M **MORE AND MORE DETERMINED** TO FINISH THE LIST WITH YOU!
IF YOU STILL WANT ME, I... **I THINK I CAN MAKE IT.**
DORIAN... IS EVERYTHING ALL RIGHT? YOU'VE BEEN ACTING WEIRD...
TOO QUIET. **ALMOST** LIKE A NORMAL PERSON. I'M NOT USED TO IT.
DOC... THERE ARE **THINGS YOU NEED TO KNOW.**
YOU WON'T HAVE TO ASK PERSONAL QUESTIONS, SO YOU WON'T BREAK THE PROMISE.
COME ON, TELL ME.
W-WE... I--
THE LIST! IT LOOKS LIKE IT'S IMPOSSIBLE TO FINISH IT.
OH-- YOU CHECKED HOW IT ENDS?
CAN I SEE...?

"--AND DO SOMETHING TRUE. SOMETHING THAT WILL MAKE REALITY BETTER THAN ANY MOVIE."
SO... OUR LAST STOP IS BACK HOME.
EXACTLY. HOME TO BLOW THAT ABSURD LAST MISSION.
DORIAN, I'M SURE YOU WILL FIND A PERFECT WAY TO FULFILL THIS LAST POINT.
DON'T TORTURE YOURSELF THIS WAY. WE ARE GONNA COMPLETE THIS LIST!
COMPLETE THIS LIST...
REMEMBER, I'M WITH YOU! YOU'RE NOT ALONE IN THIS!
LET'S SEE, FIRST OF ALL... WHAT WILL THEY MEAN BY TRUTH?
I DON'T KNOW. MY BROTHER WAS ALWAYS A BIG DREAMER...
YOUR BROTHER...?
DORIAN... THERE'S MORE YOU WANT TO TELL ME, ISN'T THERE?
...SIGH

SO... Y-YOU, TOO, COULD...?
ISN'T THERE A TEST? THERE MUST BE. TELL ME THERE'S A TEST.
IF YOU CAN'T AFFORD IT I CAN TAKE CARE OF THAT-
DOC, DOC... IT'S OK
W-WE MUST GET BACK HOME NOW. NO, WAIT! MAYBE WE CAN GET YOU TESTED HERE--
DOC, I WON'T GET TESTED.
WHAT? WHY?

WELL, THIS ONE IS A PERSONAL QUESTION. AND I DON'T LIKE IT.
DORIAN, I'M A DOCTOR! AND I CARE ABOUT YOU! WHAT WERE YOU EXPECTING ME TO SAY??
YEAH. I REALLY DON'T KNOW WHAT I WAS EXPECTING.
WHAT—WHERE- DORIAN, PLEASE!
JUST FUCKING STOP!
YOU MUST GET TESTED! MAYBE THERE IS STILL SOMETHING THAT CAN BE DONE!
AND YOU WILL KNOW IT WHEN IT'S TOO LATE ONLY BECAUSE YOU'RE TOO MUCH OF A COWARD TO FIND OUT?
WAS THIS WHAT THAT PROMISE WAS ABOUT? NOT MAKING ANY OF US FEEL ENTITLED TO PASS JUDGMENT ON THE OTHER?
I SHOULD HAVE TAKEN IT MORE SERIOUSLY, THEN.
BECAUSE SOMEONE LIKE YOU SURELY COULDN'T WAIT TO PASS JUDGMENT ON MY CHOICES.
ARE YOU MAKING THIS ABOUT ME, NOW?? JUST BECAUSE I'M WORRIED FOR YOU?

WE ARE VERY DIFFERENT, DOC. I DON'T HAVE THE LEAST INTENTION OF KNOWING WHAT'S WAITING FOR ME.
IF IT HAS TO HAPPEN, IT WILL. BUT WHEN THE MOMENT COMES, I WILL HAVE NOTHING TO REGRET. I WON'T HAVE SPENT THE MOST OF THE TIME I HAVE LEFT IN AN HOSPITAL, TRYING TO SLOW DOWN THE INEVITABLE.
I WANT TO ENJOY EVERY SINGLE BREATH, DO YOU UNDERSTAND THAT? I WANT THE WIND ON MY FACE, EVERY ROAD OPEN AHEAD FOR MY FEET TO WALK ON. THE FREEDOM TO SEE EVERYTHING I HAVEN'T SEEN YET.
I WANT EVERY NEW EMOTION. THE GOOD ONES, THE BAD ONES... I WANT TO TRY EVERYTHING!
TO JUDGE WHAT A MOVIE HAS TO SAY YOU MUST NECESSARILY WATCH UNTIL THE END, DON'T YOU THINK? IF ONLY JUST TO KNOW WHAT IT TRULY IS ABOUT.
AND EVERYTHING WE LIVE, WHEN DO WE GET TO ITS MEANING? HOW DO YOU KNOW WHEN THE END OF THE STORY IS NEAR? MY WHOLE LIFE I'VE BEEN WAITING FOR A SIGN.
I'M TIRED, DOC. I WON'T WAIT FOR THE END, I WON'T EXPECT TO UNDERSTAND ANYTHING, I JUST WANT TO LIVE. I WANT TO LIVE NOW.
ARE YOU EVEN LISTENING TO YOURSELF?? DORIAN! YOU DON'T LIVE IN A MOVIE. THIS IS REALITY!
YOU CAN'T JUST ENJOY THE MOMENT WITHOUT ANY KIND OF PLAN! LIFE MUST HAVE A SERIES OF OBJECTIVES, OF HIGH GOALS! OTHERWISE, W-WHAT'S THE MEANING OF EVERYTHING...?
HOW CAN YOU PLAN ANYTHING IF YOU DON'T KNOW HOW MUCH TIME YOU HAVE?

ARE YOU JEALOUS, DOC? JUST BECAUSE YOU WOULDN'T BE ABLE TO LIVE LIKE IN THE MOVIES?
I DON'T GET YOU... YOU HAVE LOADS OF MONEY, AND YOU TOLD ME THAT YOU HAVEN'T DONE PRACTICALLY ANYTHING TO ENJOY THEM UNTIL NOW. I DON'T WANT THIS KIND OF NON-LIFE YOU HAVE! I DON'T WANT TO LOSE MYSELF RUNNING AFTER AN OBJECTIVE THAT WOULD DEPRIVE ME OF EVERYTHING ELSE THERE IS IN LIFE!
SURE, YOU'RE GETTING BETTER... BUT WOULD YOU GO ON LIKE THIS IF YOU WERE BY YOURSELF? WOULD YOU BE ABLE TO SAY "TO HELL WITH IT" AND JUST ENJOY LIFE?
WOULD YOU BE CAPABLE OF A GRAND GESTURE, LIKE THE ONES IN THE MOVIES? STRONG, SPONTANEOUS, UNEXPECTED? SOMETHING THAT WOULD MAKE YOU FEEL REALLY ALIVE?
CONGRATULATIONS, WHAT A MATURE CONCEPT!
LUCKILY, BESIDES YOU FREE SPIRITS WHO DON'T CARE ABOUT THE FUTURE OR ANY OTHER DAMN THING FOR THAT MATTER, THERE ALSO ARE PEOPLE WHO ARE NOT COMPLETELY SELF-ABSORBED AND DEDICATE THEMSELVES TO MAKE THINGS BETTER!
SO I'M SELFISH, TOO... GOD. DON'T YOU SEE I HAVE NOTHING LEFT TO LOSE?
DORIAN...
REALLY... NOTHING?
NOTHING.

WELL THEN... SINCE THIS IS WHAT WE THINK OF EACH OTHER, I FIGURE OUR JOURNEY TOGETHER ENDS HERE.
I WISH YOU GOOD LUCK, DORIAN.
I'M GOING BACK HOME. I'LL TRY TO BRING ORDER TO MY TEDIOUS "NON-LIFE."
RIIIP
I DON'T NEED YOU! THERE ARE NIGHT BUSES TO THE AIRPORT!
IT'S TRUE. I KNEW YOU WOULD GIVE UP! IT WAS JUST A MATTER OF TIME!
AND THIS TIME I WON'T INSIST ON ANYTHING!
WONDERFUL!
HAVE A NICE TRIP HOME, MAG!

to CDG
VRRROOM

MISS! WE ARE LEAVING!
ONE MORE MINUTE, PLEASE!
UHM-- OK, BUT THEN WE LEAVE!

VRRROOM

I AM DOCTOR MAGDALENE TRÄUMER. I JUST DID THE ONLY SENSIBLE THING TO DO AND YET I FEEL LIKE AN IDIOT.
VRRRRMM
I NEED TO GATHER ALL OF MY ABILITY IN SCIENTIFIC DATA ANALYSIS. BECAUSE IT IS UNDOUBTEDLY A MATTER I EXCEL IN. UNLIKE HUMAN RELATIONS.
PREMISE: A LIFE PLAN IS NECESSARY. STRAIGHT TO THE GOAL. FOCUSED. THE WAY I USED TO LIVE.
RESULT: THE UNPREDICTABLE HAPPENS AND MAKES YOUR HOUSE OF CARDS FALL. YOUR SACRIFICES WILL PROBABLY SERVE THE RICH WHO WANT TO MAKE EVEN MORE MONEY AND NOT THOSE WHOSE LIVES YOU MEANT TO SAVE. YOU FIND YOURSELF BACK AT THE STARTING POINT.
DATA. I NEED MORE DATA.
-NO LONGER VIABLE OPTION: GOING BACK AND WASTE MORE TIME WITH THAT INCONSIDERATE, RECKLESS WOMAN. A TIME THAT COULD BE PRECIOUS TO THE WORLD. ENERGIES MY BRILLIANT MIND SHOULD USE IN THE SERVICE OF HUMANKIND.
-DOUBT: IS THIS WHAT I WANT TO BE? JUST A TOOL? WHAT IF THERE IS A WAY TO COMBINE THE TWO THINGS? TO FIND A MIDDLE WAY? I'D LIKE TO HAVE THE TIME TO FIND IT.
STAY FOCUSED. MAGDALENE.
I... I WOULDN'T GET TO SEE HER AGAIN. I WOULDN'T BE THERE WHEN SHE FINDS A SOLUTION FOR THAT LAST ISSUE ON THE LIST. WHEN SHE LAUGHS FOR THE LAST TIME. WHEN SHE-- DO I REALLY WANT TO MISS THIS?
NO. DATA. DATA ONLY. ONLY THE REAL HEART OF THE PROBLEM. WHAT IS THE HEART OF THE PROBLEM?

DAMN, MAGDALENE. ARE YOU REALLY GOING TO DENY THIS HAS BEEN THE HAPPIEST TIME OF YOUR LIFE?
BUT... HOW DO YOU PERSUADE A COMPLETELY UNPREDICTABLE WOMAN TO FORGIVE YOU?
NO, NO. I KNOW WHAT TO DO. AND YOU DON'T NEED A BRILLIANT MIND TO GET IT...
I JUST HAVE TO PROVE THAT, NO MATTER WHAT SHE SAYS, I AM CAPABLE OF GRAND GESTURES.
COME ON, MAGDALENE, YOU CAN DO IT TOO!
VROOOOOOOOOOO...

Terminal 1
ZOOOM

EXCUSE ME! EXCUSE ME, PLEASE!!
PLEASE TELL ME YOU'RE STILL HERE!!
AH!
MISS! YOU NEED TO SWIPE YOUR BOARDING PASS ON THE SCANNER!
I-I... PLEASE, I AM IN DIRE NEED OF A GRAND GESTURE!! DON'T YOU SEE?
C-CAN I GO?

DIN!
Shuttle Bus

Shuttle Bus
YES!

DORIAN!! I'M HERE!
(WHAT'S ALL THIS SCREAMING ABOUT?)
(THIS AIRPORT WASN'T A MADHOUSE ONCE!)
I-I...
JUST LIKE IN THE MOVIES, MAGDALENE. LIKE IN THE MOVIES.
DAMN, I CAN DO IT!
DORIAN! PLEASE STOP!!

I-- BEGAN THIS CRAZY ADVENTURE WITH YOU AND I WANT TO FINISH IT WITH YOU!
PLEASE, ALLOW ME! GET BACK TO TRAVELING WITH ME AGAIN!
ARRIVALS
B13

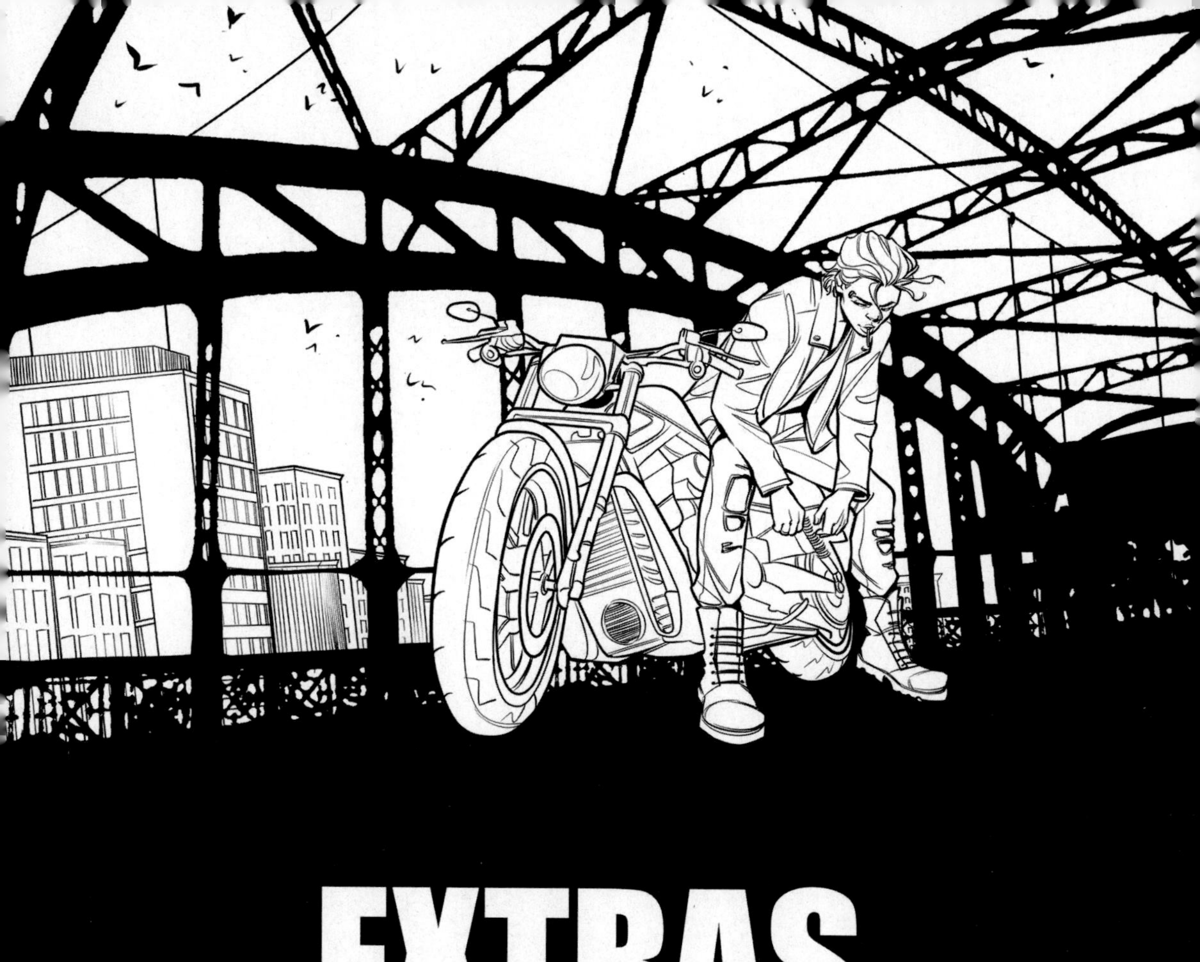

EXTRAS

Issue #1 Cover C art by MIRKA ANDOLPHO

Issue #1 Cover Z art by IVAN TAO

Issue #2 Cover C by ELISA and IOLANDA

Issue #3 Cover C by ELISA and IOLANDA

Character studies

Cover processes

Issue #1 Cover A pencils to inks. (Final colored version on page 5)

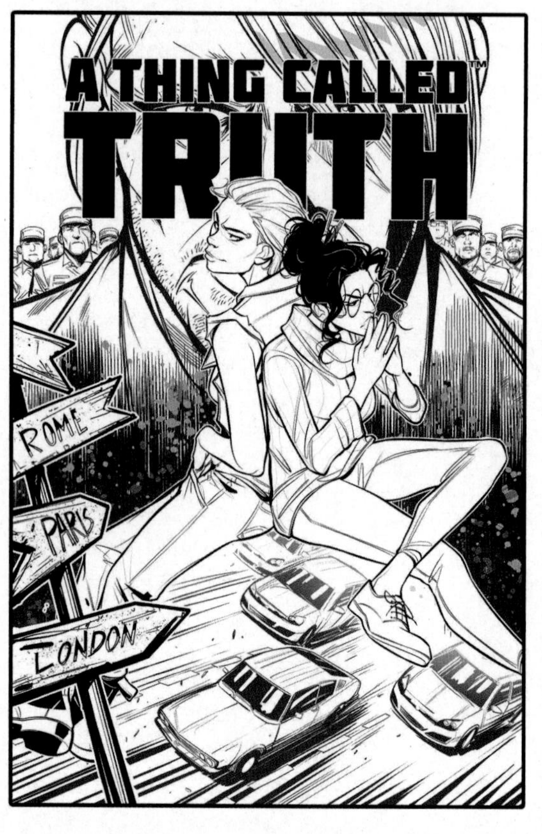

Issue #4 Cover C fron sketch to inks. (Final colored version on page 4)

Pencils for Issue #3 Covers A and B. (
Final colored versions on pages 53 and 54)

Rejected cover sketches for issue #2.
Check pages 29, 30 and 128-129 to see how this idea was improved on.

From drama to fantasy, comedy to horror,satire to sci-fi...

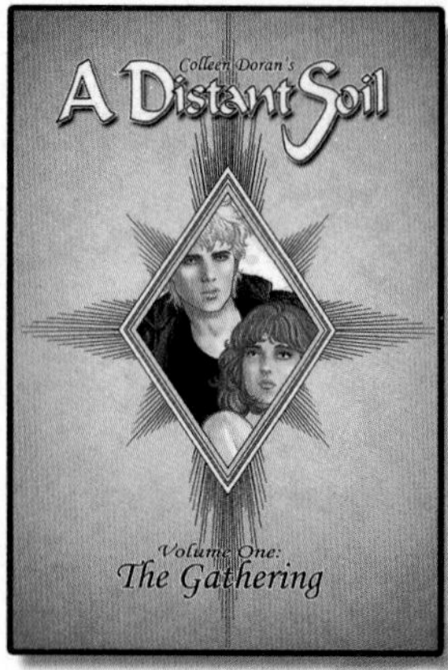

A DISTANT SOIL

Colleen Doran's legendary magnum opus completely remastered and re-edited with beautiful new die-cut covers. Two volumes.

A THING CALLED TRUTH

A chaotic road trip through Europe may lead a workaholic scientist and a woman who appears absolutely fearless to an unexpected romance.

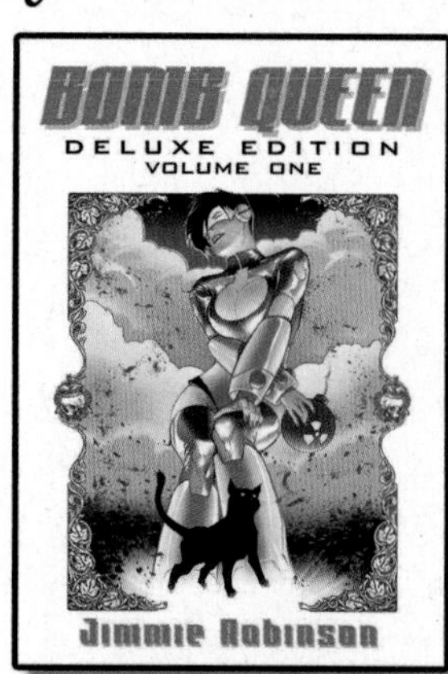

BOMB QUEEN DELUXE

Jimmie Robinson's adults only satire of politics, sex and social mores. Not for the easily offended! Four Oversize hardcover volumes.

COMPLETE normalman

The legendary classic parody series collected into a single gigantic volume for the first time!

COWBOY NINJA VIKING

Now in a Deluxe Oversize hardcover edition! Duncan has three distinct personalities.. So, of course he's been made a government agent!

DIA DE LOS MUERTOS

Nine acclaimed writers and one amazing artist, Riley Rossmo, tell tales from the Mexican Day of the Dead.

THE EMPTY

Tanoor finds a chance to save her people when a stranger with the power to grow life from death drifts into her empty, decaying town.

FASTER THAN LIGHT

In the near future we discove the secret to faster than ligh travel. The whole universe i opened to us, but are w ready for it? Two volumes.

FIVE WEAPONS

In a school for assassins, Tyler has the greatest of them all going for him...his mind!
Two volumes by Jimmie Robinson!

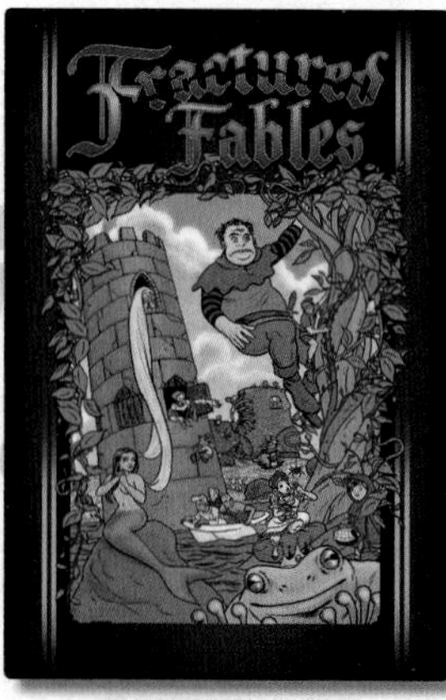

FRACTURED FABLES

Over 50 award winning cartoonists take old Fairy Tales and turn them on their ear! Superbly illustrated and fun for everyone!

GREEN WAKE Vol. I & II

A riveting tale of loss and horror that blends mystery and otherworldly eccentricity in two unforgettable, critically acclaimed volumes.

HARVEST

Welcome to Dr. Benjamin Dane's nightmare. His only way out? Bring down the man who set him up by reclaiming illegally harvested organs.